Jessie's Winning Streak

PATRINA McKENNA

This book is a work of fiction. Names, characters, places, and incidents either are products of the author's imagination or are used fictitiously. Any resemblance to actual persons, living or dead, events, or locales is entirely coincidental.

Publisher: Patrina McKenna

patrina.mckenna@outlook.com

ISBN-13: 978-1-8381827-5-5

Also by Patrina McKenna

Romantic comedy with a twist!

Truelove Hills
Truelove Hills – Mystery at Pebble Cove
Truelove Hills – The Matchmaker
Granny Prue's Bucket List
Christmas with the Neighbours
Trouble at Featherlow Forbes Menswear
Lady Featherlow's Tea Room
Christmas in Featherlow Bottom
Weddings by Saffronella
Millie's Change of Fortune
Jessie's Winning Streak

Feel good fantasy for all the family!

GIANT Gemstones
A Galaxy of Gemstones
The Gemstone Dynasty
Enrico's Journey
Summer Camp at Tadgers Blaney Manor

DEDICATION

For my family and friends

1

TEAM EVENT

Jessie dropped her gold-plated pen on the boardroom table in disgust. How could Emilio even consider closing the office for three days while the team went on a "jolly" to reflect on their lives? Didn't he know that real estate didn't wait?

Emilio's heart sank at the sea of disgruntled faces. He was hoping not to use the "sweetener" he had up his sleeve, but he was under no doubt his highly ambitious team would change their minds about taking a break when they had a prize to fight for. He ran a hand through his sleek black hair as his brown eyes darted around the room. 'I know that taking three days out of the business may impact your commission payments this month, but there's a good chance you'll benefit in other ways.'

Piers sat back in his chair before challenging Emilio, 'How can you substantiate that?'

Emilio leaned forward on the table. 'I've asked the lead Training Consultant to assess who performs best. When the winner is identified to me, they will be given a ten-million-pound listing due to hit my inbox any day now.'

Piers pursed his lips and rocked back and forth in his chair. That made the course worthwhile. The listing would surely go to him; ten-million-pound listings were just a drop in the ocean compared to some he'd reeled in over the years.

Guy passed a note to Nate:

Let's just humour Emilio. We can work during the course. He won't know. I've got deals to close.

Nate nodded to Guy, then surprised their colleagues by siding with the boss. 'Emilio's right. We're all burnt out. A short break away will do us a power of good. When does the course start?'

Emilio sat back in his chair. 'On Wednesday next week. The course is residential, and you'll receive details by close of play today.'

*

Jessie manoeuvred her car through the leafy Cotswold

lanes. She was more used to driving through London than having to give way to horses and cattle on the roads. Jessie couldn't believe that Guy and Nate were so up for this. She was also surprised that Piers had mellowed at the news of the ten-million-pound listing; he already had higher ones on his books.

As the latest member of *Rawlinson's Residential*, Jessie's listings were all less than a million. She slammed her foot on the brake when a pheasant ran into the road, then let out a sigh of relief when she saw it fly past her windscreen. Her thoughts returned to the prize. It wasn't about how good you were at the job but about how good you were on the course. Jessie's pale blue eyes sparkled. For once, she could give her colleagues a run for their money.

*

Guy and Nate chose to drive to the Cotswolds together – a choice Nate was already regretting. Guy had been on his phone for the whole journey, while Nate had to concentrate on an intricate route leading them over a very narrow bridge and out into the open countryside. It was a dark and dreary November evening, and the sound of Guy's constant cheery banter with his clients was grating on Nate like never before. To think of it, Guy didn't come up for air in the office; it was just more noticeable in the confined space of Nate's car. Nate turned his attention to the prize this week and vowed that, when *he'd* won the listing, he'd use the extra commission to hire a yacht for his upcoming big birthday bash.

*

At thirty-nine, Piers was already thinking of retirement. What a stroke of luck his great aunt had passed away and named him the sole inheritor in her Will. That was the easiest six million pounds he'd come across. He'd had to work like a trojan to amass his current fortune. Maybe now was the time to think of slowing down and enjoying his wealth. Piers turned off the ignition of his Porsche and glanced up at the imposing manor house. He had to admit it looked a bit bleak on a dark November evening, more like the place to host a Halloween party; there must be ghosts and ghouls on demand in a place like this.

Piers checked his reflection in his rear-view mirror. He was pleased he'd gone for that spray tan yesterday. His green eyes stood out from his clean-shaven, well-moisturised face. His dark-brown hair looked great after the designer cut he'd treated himself to at the weekend in Mayfair. Piers had worn jeans and a white silk shirt for the journey but brought three Saville Row suits with him for the course. He grinned; the lead Training Consultant wouldn't be able to resist him. The commission from this latest listing meant another significant amount heading for his bank account in the coming days.

*

Jessie wheeled her case down the rickety corridor of the old musty building. She wasn't impressed with the venue for the course. Surely the training organisation could have booked something more modern? She was even less amused when Guy and Nate dragged their cases behind her. There were ten agents from *Rawlinson's Residential* on the course. Why on earth had she been given a room near to those two? Guy was an annoying joker, and Nate was his trusty sidekick. Just because she was younger than them, it didn't mean she was inferior. She was twenty-five years old, and they were both pushing thirty. That wasn't enough of an age gap to make a difference.

Nate flashed a white smile at Jessie. 'Love the hair-do. You suit it short.'

Guy grinned. 'It makes you look sophisticated. Let's hope your new image helps you bring in the listings.' Guy's smile faded as he offered Jessie some advice, 'You've been an agent for six months now, and you need to make a mark soon or Emilio will be questioning why he took you on.'

Nate smiled at Jessie before glaring at Guy. 'That's a bit harsh. It takes time to build relationships and bring the listings in.'

Guy shrugged his shoulders. 'Don't I know that?

I'm just warning Jessie this is a cutthroat business. If any of us are to get on, we need to remove Mr Cool over there.' Jessie followed Guy's gaze, which had turned to witness the agency's tanned top performer wheeling a suitcase down the dimly lit corridor.

Piers saluted to his colleagues before closing his bedroom door behind him. Guy raised his eyes to the ceiling. 'See that? He acts like he's our Commanding Officer. He'll be a nightmare this week without Emilio here to keep him in check. If he decides to inspect our rooms, I'll be in trouble. I'll be living out of my suitcase; I never bother to unpack when I'm on holiday.'

Jessie glared at Guy. 'You're not on holiday. We're still at work, and I understand your point about proving myself. I'm doing my best. I've got two listings of just under a million on my books at the moment, and I have high hopes of closing them soon. It's just a pain that we have to go under the radar with our clients for three days.'

Nate raised his eyes to the ceiling. 'Tell me about it. There are, however, ways and means to keep on top of our listings while we're here.'

Jessie frowned. 'How?'

Guy couldn't believe that Jessie was being so stupid. 'There'll be breaks; we'll have our iPhones on us at all times; we can ping off a few contracts and emails in the evenings when we return to our rooms. The only thing we won't be able to do is site visits, which will mean jam-packed schedules for us all next week.'

Jessie tutted before reminding her colleagues of the purpose of the course, 'That's not the instruction from Emilio. We're supposed to switch off entirely from work for three days – and nights. There's no way either of you will win the ten-million-pound listing.' Jessie opened her bedroom door before smiling over her shoulder, 'So carry on with your plans, boys. My eyes are on the prize.'

2

ROLES REVEALED

Jessie crossed her legs and folded her arms. Just her luck, she was sandwiched between Piers on her right and Guy and Nate on her left. She was surprised they were all wearing suits when the Dress Code for the course was Smart Casual. For her part, she had chosen to wear a pale pink cashmere sweater and black jeans. Wearing her favourite black suede ankle boots rather than uncomfortable stilettos made a nice change.

Piers checked his phone before switching off the sound and dropping it into his jacket pocket. Guy and Nate kept one eye on the door and the other on their phones, which they held under the table as they sent last-minute messages before the course commenced. Piers was wearing his latest expensive aftershave today.

He was pleased he'd secured a place in the front row. The trainer wouldn't be able to resist his natural charm. Smelling good would be a bonus; he'd try to sit next to her at lunch. Every little helped when there was a prize to be won.

The door to the conference room flew open, and a smiling, dark-haired man bounded inside. He placed an armful of papers on the table at the front of the room and stood with hands on hips. 'Hi, everyone. My name's Luca, and I'm your trainer.' Piers sank back in his chair; he had no intention of winning Luca around with his manly charms; he'd need to think of a different tactic.

Luca passed a set of papers around the room. 'I understand you all work in real estate. Taking time out of the business to go on a boring three-day course will be painful for you – not forgetting the adverse effect it will have on your commission payments. With that in mind, I want to ease you into the course by doing something you're accustomed to.'

Guy pinged off an email under the table and whispered to Nate, 'What's he going on about?' Jessie cringed when she noticed Luca's body stiffen beneath his friendly exterior. Guy and Nate were just so rude. Piers was also lounging in his chair, looking deflated.

Luca's soft brown eyes focused on Jessie's chest. She folded her arms even tighter, then realised her name badge was lopsided. She straightened it up, and Luca smiled at her. 'Jessie. I want you to pretend you're the Lady of the Manor.'

Jessie gulped. 'Which manor?'

Luca's smile didn't waiver. 'This manor. Hinchingthorpe Manor.'

Piers held a finger in the air. 'OK, I'll be the Lord. That'll suit me to the ground.'

Luca shook his head. 'No need. The Lady doesn't need a Lord on this occasion. She needs a gardener, though. That will be your role.'

Before a red-faced Piers could complain, Luca turned his attention to Guy and Nate. 'You two are brothers who have just won the lottery and are looking for an investment opportunity.' Luca waved an arm around the room. 'The rest of you don't need to act; just do your day jobs. Take a look around the building and establish its selling points. You are working for the Lady, and you need to persuade the lottery winners to splash their cash on buying this relic of a place. We'll have a debate later.'

Jessie put her hand up. 'But what if I don't want to sell?'

Luca's eyes twinkled. 'The scenario can take multiple directions. Let's see how it goes.' He reached for a box under the table and placed it on top. 'You should all become acquainted with the manor. View it from the eyes of the characters you've been given. Embrace the role play and see where it leads.' Luca held the box aloft. 'We'll meet in the restaurant for lunch at one o'clock. Place your mobile phones in here as you leave the room. No Googling allowed on this occasion. Not everything about this place is online. You need to find the hidden traits.'

A refreshment area was outside the conference room with self-service drinks and a selection of cakes and Danish pastries. Guy and Nate sat down with their coffees. Nate was agitated. 'I can't believe we've been made to give up our phones. How ridiculous. I feel like my right arm's missing.'

Guy took a bite out of a jam doughnut before licking his lips. 'Well, my right arm's well and truly in place.' He patted his trouser pocket. 'I can't believe you did what Lucky Luca asked.'

'Why's he Lucky Luca?'

'Because he's got a doddle of a job making fun of us. He can't keep the smile off his face.'

Nate chuckled. 'You must admit it was funny when he chose Piers to be the gardener.'

Guy grinned. 'Now, that might not be a bad role if Piers plays it correctly. Remember Lady Chatterley's Lover?'

Nate sighed. 'That was the gamekeeper, not the gardener.'

Guy shrugged before taking his phone out of his pocket to check his messages. 'Same thing.'

Jessie headed straight for the Reception. She smiled at the elderly lady behind the desk, whose name badge read: *MARIA – Head Receptionist.* 'Hello, Maria. My name's Jessie. I'm here on a course, and I need to know a bit about the manor's history and its facilities. For example, how many bedrooms, bathrooms, square footage, acres of land etc. Also, when it was last sold and how much for? Would you be able to help me?'

Maria frowned. 'I don't know that type of stuff. I know the story of the murdered gardener, though. He haunts the cricket pavilion to this very day.'

Jessie shuddered before gaining her composure. 'The grounds must be large if a cricket pitch has a pavilion. Are there tennis courts? A swimming pool?'

Maria nodded. 'Yes, we have all those.'

Jessie glanced up at the portraits adorning the staircase. 'Is there currently a Lady of the Manor?'

Maria shook her head. 'No, dear. The Lady left years ago.'

Maria lowered her eyes, and Jessie sensed her questioning was hitting a brick wall. 'Well, thank you. You've been very helpful. I'll take one of these brochures so I can familiarise myself with the venue's facilities.'

Piers sat in his car and took his spare phone out of the glove compartment. What a waste of three days. Was the ten-million-pound listing even worth it? Emilio wasn't in his right mind to send the team on this shambolic excuse of a course.

Luca could tell from the start which participants were open to expanding their minds and trying new things. As his brother, Emilio, had advised him, several members of *Rawlinson's Residential* were closed off. It wasn't good to be blinkered – for the individual or the organisation. Luca went to speak to Maria at Reception. Hi, Mamma. How many of them have come to gain some expert knowledge from you?'

Maria's brown eyes twinkled. 'Just the nice blonde lady – Jessie – I like her.'

3

BECOMING ACQUAINTED

There was a tap on Piers' car window. He lifted his head to see a stunning raven-haired woman with large shiny brown eyes staring at him. Piers ended the call with a client and opened his car door before stepping outside and reading her name badge. 'Good morning, Sophia. What can I do for you?'

Sophia was agitated. 'It's the chauffeur again. We've had a mass exodus from the West Wing.' Sophia threw her arms in the air. 'What are we going to do?'

Piers was intrigued by this beautiful damsel who was obviously in distress. He took hold of her hand and linked it through his arm before turning the sound off his spare phone and locking it in his car. 'There's no need to worry now I'm here. Tell me all about the chauffeur, and I'll help you find a solution to your concerns. I have nothing else to do today.'

*

Jessie had a spring in her step as she headed for the cricket pavilion. She grinned at the thought of the ghost. The staff at the venue were all part of a spoof. They must host murder mystery weekends here too. Jessie needed to focus her mind; she had to admit this was a bizarre course. By the time she reached the pavilion, it was starting to rain, and she'd left her coat in her room. She soon concluded that venturing so far from the manor house hadn't been a good idea. For one thing, a damp cashmere sweater would feel uncomfortable all afternoon.

Jessie turned the handle on the door to the pavilion and was relieved to find it was unlocked. At least she could wait in the dry until the rain stopped. She lifted a plastic chair off a pile in the corner and sat down to read the brochure she'd picked up from Reception.

*

Luca held out his hand, and Guy handed his phone over. Nate leaned back in his chair with a coffee and felt smug that he'd conformed to the trainer's rules. Guy would have no chance now of winning the prize.

Luca didn't disappear; instead, he hovered over the "lottery winners" until they became uncomfortable. They didn't appear to know where to start with the task they'd been set, so Luca decided to give them a nudge. 'Now, if I'd won the lottery, I'd be keen to make the money work for me. I'd find an investment opportunity and go all out to ensure I secured the deal. This place could be an absolute cash cow if the new owners had vision and drive.'

Guy held his shoulders back. 'We have vision and drive, don't we, Nate?'

Nate placed his empty coffee mug on the table before standing up. 'We certainly do.'

Luca gave them more guidance. 'There's no guarantee the Lady will sell her home to you. Why are you wasting time when you could be working on a proposal she can't refuse?'

Guy grinned. 'That's where you've got your wires crossed, mate. We're the buyers, and most of our team are in their usual roles as estate agents – all the work's down to them. Thanks for giving us an easy day!'

Luca raised an eyebrow, and Nate sensed his dissatisfaction at their nonchalance. 'Well, I suppose we could look about the place and maybe buy the Lady a coffee to get us in her good books.'

Guy's eyes lit up. 'We're missing the obvious here. If we get to the Lady before the estate agents with an offer she can't refuse, then she won't have to pay them commission, and we'll get the property at a knocked-down price. It's all about thinking out of the box. I'm starting to see where this course is going.' Guy turned to Luca. 'Did you see which way Jessie went?'

Luca nodded towards the window. 'The Lady's in the cricket pavilion.'

Guy winked at Luca. 'Thanks for the tip off. You've given us lots of food for thought.'

Nate smiled. 'Yes. Thanks, Luca. You couldn't have chosen a better couple to identify investment opportunities for this place. We'll meet up with the Lady straight away for a brainstorming session.'

Luca waved as he headed off, and Guy and Nate viewed the torrential rain through the window. There was no point going outside to get drenched. Jessie was their friend, and they'd easily get her to sell the manor to them directly rather than go through their fellow estate agents. Easy peasy, time for a pre-lunch beer.

*

Rain was lashing down now, and Jessie was becoming worried. What if it didn't stop before one o'clock? She couldn't get back to the main building without a coat or umbrella and had no phone to contact anyone. A shiver ran down her spine. No one would think of looking for her in the cricket pavilion. Jessie placed the brochure on a table and went to stand by a window. The sky darkened before a rumble of thunder, and then a flash of forked lightning lit up the inside of the pavilion. Jessie screamed when the brochure flew to the floor. There must be a window open somewhere. She turned to see it wasn't an open window – it was the door.

*

Piers walked the entire length of the West Wing with Sophia gripping his arm. 'You'll have to tell me what we're looking for. If the chauffeur has been bothering people, I'll sort him out. I'm a karate black belt.'

Sophia shook her head. 'Only a gardener can sort him out.'

Piers let out a massive chuckle. 'You have to be kidding me? This is some sort of a farce. Well, you can't fool me. I haven't got to where I am today without smelling a rat.'

Sophia's eyes were ablaze. 'Would *you* buy a place like this?'

Piers frowned. 'Is it on the market?'

Sophia lowered her eyes. 'Not yet.'

Piers always took advantage of every opportunity; he reached inside his jacket pocket and produced a card. 'Here are my details. Contact me as soon as you hear of the property coming up for sale. Let me buy you a coffee, and you can tell me all about the troublesome chauffeur.'

Sitting beside a roaring fire in the bar area, Sophia began to relax. Piers had ordered coffees laced with brandy, and Sophia couldn't help but be impressed by the undivided attention of this charming man who was more interested in spending time with her than being on a course. 'Now tell me what the chauffeur's done.'

'He picks flowers from the gardens and gives them to his girlfriend.'

Piers raised his eyebrows. 'Isn't that a nice thing to do?'

Sophia shook her head. 'Not when the gardener's just raked manure into the rose beds.'

Piers let out a chuckle. 'Surely, picked flowers won't smell of manure? Roses are minimal this time of the year too. Why has the chauffeur offended all the guests in the West Wing?'

'Because he gets manure on his shoes and his car whiffs of it. We've told him repeatedly, but now he's on a final warning. He carried several bags into the

West Wing last night with the smell on his shoes, and the guests have had enough. It's been three nights in a row this week.'

Piers suppressed another chuckle. 'How can a gardener help with this?'

'The gardener has a vital job. He needs to keep an eye on things outside of the manor at all times. A chauffeur trampling through manure should be a red flag to the gardener.'

Piers scratched his chin. The "gardener" role didn't seem so low after all. Maybe he had a significant part to play.

*

Jessie walked backwards into a corner of the room; she'd never been so frightened in her life! The wind was whistling around the pavilion; forks of lightning lit up the sky, and the brochure that had blown onto the floor was moving! The door flung fully open, and Jessie screamed before throwing a hand to her chest. 'Emilio! Thank goodness it's you!'

Emilio's brown eyes shone as he shook his umbrella and handed Jessie a coat. 'This will be too big, but I wanted to keep you dry. Come with me. I have something important for you to do.'

4

WHISKED AWAY

Emilio glanced over his shoulder as he waited outside Jessie's room. 'Be quick. We need to leave before one o'clock.'

Jessie zipped up her case. 'What will everyone say when I don't turn up for lunch?'

'They won't even notice.'

Jessie handed Emilio the coat as she closed her bedroom door. 'Thanks for the loan of this.' Emilio threw the coat over his shoulder and grabbed Jessie's case. He wasn't surprised to see her frown before questioning him, 'What do you mean "they won't even notice"?'

Emilio glanced sideways at Jessie as they rushed down the corridor. 'They're all too interested in themselves to think about anyone else. Luca knows you're safe with me. That's all that matters.'

'Where are we going?'

'To Paris.'

'Paris?!'

'Yes. My girlfriend's in bed with the flu. There's no way I'm going to a cocktail party alone.'

'A cocktail party?! I have nothing to wear.'

'Don't worry about that. My girlfriend's arranged for a selection of outfits to be available in your room. I had to guess your size. Now, keep your head down until we get in the car.'

Jessie's eyes widened when she saw a chauffeur bending down outside a silver Bentley changing his shoes. 'Good morning, Mr Hinchingthorpe.'

Emilio laughed. 'I see you've been playing along with Sophia's plan. You're a good sport, Charles. Did you manage to get Piers to catch you in the act?'

'I certainly did, Sir. Miss Sophia managed to keep a straight face throughout. She's a born actress, that one.'

Emilio grinned as he helped Jessie into the backseat of the car. 'Charles, this is Jessie. She's not a good actress, so I had to rescue her from the course and take her to Paris. She'll be back in time for the prize giving on Friday.'

Jessie's head was spinning. Why did Charles call Emilio "Mr Hinchingthorpe"? His name was Emilio Rawlinson. Emilio certainly seemed very "at home" here. He knew Charles, Luca, and "Miss Sophia".

The Bentley cruised down the drive and headed for the airport. Emilio felt Jessie's eyes burning into the side of his head. He took out a notepad and wrote down a message which he held out for her to read:

I'll explain everything
when we're in private.

Jessie nodded and stared out of the window while wrestling with her thoughts.

*

It was one o'clock, and the delegates tucked into lunch in the dining room. Guy glanced at Piers. 'What's up with you? You can't keep the smile off your face.'

Piers tapped his nose. 'The gardener has the most important role in this. I've already made a significant difference this morning.'

Nate looked up from his pepperoni pizza; he had to admit the food selection for lunch hit the right spot. It was the best thing about the course so far. Piers had a twinkle in his eye and was no doubt waiting for someone to question why he'd "made a difference". Nate took the bait. 'What have you done to make a difference?'

Piers sat back in his chair and folded his arms behind his head. 'I've sacked the chauffeur.'

Guy spluttered before placing his glass on the table. 'Why did you sack the chauffeur?'

'Because no one here has dared to do so. The chauffeur's misdemeanours have been going on for far too long.'

Nate gulped. 'But you don't have the authority to sack a chauffeur. We're here on a course; you're just pretending to be the gardener for a day. Luca will have a lot to say about this when he finds out.'

Piers puffed out his chest. 'Well, Sophia was pleased with me. She said I was "incredible". As far as I'm concerned, I've won the prize. By dealing with a major problem head-on, I've increased the future revenue potential for the manor. Remember what Luca said: "The Lady needs a gardener, not a Lord". The clue was in that very sentence. I was given the most important role, and I smashed it.'

Luca entered the dining room and sat down at an adjacent table. Piers waved to him. 'As requested, we all arrived here for lunch at one o'clock. What's the plan for this afternoon? I'm ahead of the game with my achievement from this morning. If your plans are loose, then I'll dip out of the course this afternoon as I have the potential to do more good deeds for a member of staff.'

Luca kept his calm. How could his brother work with people like this? He placed his beef burrito on a plate and wiped his hands on a serviette. 'We have a full afternoon of activities planned. Everyone needs to be back in the conference room by two o'clock.'

Luca turned to chat to the delegates on his table, and Guy decided to question Piers, 'OK, if it was *you* who'd won the lottery, what would you do with this place?'

Nate grinned at Guy. What a great idea to get Piers to do their job for them. *He'd* come up with a whole raft of suggestions. All Nate had thought of so far was a spa hotel, and Guy was angling for a casino.

Piers rubbed his chin. 'I'd turn it into high-class apartments for the Over 60s. My great aunt was lonely in her mansion in her later years. Why have a big place for one person and a few staff? There will be lots of people like my great aunt who would be prepared to splash out on an apartment in this building. In doing so, they would become part of a community and could enjoy undertaking activities together.'

It was Nate's turn to choke on his drink. 'That's a nice idea, Piers. What activities would they do?'

Piers pursed his lips while he thought. 'Well, they could go on theatre trips, have tea dances, watch cricket. Did you know this place has a cricket pavilion? I'm quite partial to a game of cricket myself.'

*

Jessie sat in the Bentley, listening to Emilio take one business call after another. *Her* phone was still in Luca's confiscation box. When they arrived at an airfield and parked outside a private jet, Emilio switched his phone off. He looked over at Jessie. 'You don't seem very concerned about being away from the business. You were the first to complain about it when I suggested the course.'

Jessie's pale blue eyes bore into her boss. 'What do you expect? I'm in a state of shock. From having my phone confiscated, being spooked by the ghost of the murdered gardener in the cricket pavilion – well, so I thought – to being hijacked from attending a course where I was determined to win first prize. Then being bundled onto a flight to Paris for a cocktail party, knowing your girlfriend has chosen an outfit for me to wear. You must admit I've got a right not to be thinking about work.'

Emilio's eyes twinkled. 'Got it! You're worried

about the outfit.'

As soon as they were on the plane, Jessie confronted her boss, 'You need to tell me what's going on. Why did the chauffeur call you "Mr Hinchingthorpe", and why are we all on the course?'

Emilio smiled. 'It's simple. Charles likes to massage my ego – he's always telling me I'm destined for greater things. He's also quite fond of my mother, brother, and sister, who all work at Hinchingthorpe Manor. You'll have noticed the place needs a facelift. The current owners are struggling to make a success of it as a hotel and are keen to get it off their hands. It's proving difficult, though, with the rumours of murdered gardeners, ghosts, and the like.'

Jessie's eyes widened. 'Go on, tell me more.'

'I needed to find a way of getting Piers to view the property.'

'Why?'

'Because he'll buy it.'

5

IDEAS DIVULGED

With the delegates back in the conference room, Piers noticed the empty seat next to him. He turned to Guy and Nate. 'Where's Jessie?'

Guy shrugged, and Nate frowned before responding, 'She went to the cricket pavilion earlier. Come to think of it, she wasn't there at lunch.'

Guy chuckled. 'The Lady got one over on the gardener. Jessie's managed to sneak off this afternoon while Piers well and truly got slapped wrists for suggesting he'd something better to do. Well done, Jessie!'

Before Piers could argue, Sophia entered the

room. 'Hello, everyone. I'm your trainer for this afternoon's session.' Sophia smiled at Piers, and his tanned cheeks took on a reddish hue. She looked stunning standing there at the front of the room; not many women could surprise him. Sophia was something else.

Sophia glanced at the notes Luca had provided. 'I'm aware most of you have had a productive morning. Using your skills and expertise as estate agents, you've uncovered the wealth of potential Hinchingthorpe Manor has to offer. If this property ever came onto the market, buyers would be queuing down the tree-lined drive right back to the motorway.'

Guy suppressed a chuckle. Sophia was more suited to being a trainer than an estate agent; buyers wouldn't be queuing up to buy this place. Sophia continued, 'With that in mind, how have our lottery winners got on with their plans for identifying an investment opportunity?'

Nate spoke first, 'We thought of turning it into a spa hotel or maybe a casino.'

Sophia tutted. 'You haven't done your research. There are three spa hotels and a casino within a five-mile radius of the manor. There would be no demand for either of those suggestions.'

Piers put his hand up but was beaten to it by Guy,

who blurted out his suggestion to Sophia, 'We've saved our real proposal until last, just to surprise you.' Sophia's eyes widened, and Guy went to stand next to her. 'Let me borrow your whiteboard pen.' Sophia handed Guy a pen, and he drew the manor in sections: four for each of the East and West Wings. Then seven in the main house. Guy scratched his head. 'That's two lots of four and an additional seven – making fifteen apartments.'

Sophia's eyes darkened. 'You want to turn Hinchingthorpe Manor, a much-loved family home and thriving conference and wedding venue, into apartments?!'

Guy shuffled his feet. Sophia wasn't impressed. He wasn't enamoured with the idea of an Over 60's Club either, but he didn't have any suitable ideas of his own. Guy needed to come up with something, though, to be in with a chance of winning the prize. 'I'm not suggesting *any* apartments. They would be luxurious ones for the Over 60's. This place could be a family home again. All the lonely rich people who could afford an apartment would become part of a community that could go on theatre trips and play cricket.'

Piers slumped back in his chair, and Nate stood up. 'Guy shouldn't take all the credit for the idea. We're joint lottery winners and have debated our options for a sound investment all morning.'

Sophia couldn't believe the type of people Emilio worked with. Guy and Nate would sell their grandmothers to secure a deal or win a prize. Luca had overheard Piers suggest the luxury apartment idea at lunchtime, and now Guy and Nate had announced it as their own. Sophia glanced over at Piers, who remained composed even though two of his colleagues had stabbed him in the back. She couldn't help but smile at him as a thought emerged. 'Have the lottery winners spoken to the Lady about their proposal?'

Guy and Nate shook their heads, and Sophia tutted again. 'Without the Lady's presence, we cannot continue this afternoon's session.'

Nate identified an opportunity to get into the trainer's good books. He couldn't let Guy stand out from the crowd. *He* needed to make an impact too. 'I disagree. Why don't the estate agents spend this afternoon liaising with the lottery winners? We'll have all our ducks in a row when Jessie turns up again. Emilio will want to ensure we get the most out of the course. We don't need the Lady this afternoon.'

Sophia suppressed a smile. 'That's a great idea, Nate.' She glanced at Piers without connecting eyes. 'It just means the gardener will be at a loss this afternoon. I can ensure you get your phone back, Piers, so that you can make the best use of your time.'

Piers jumped up. 'That would be very kind of you.'

Sophia looked over her shoulder as she left the room with Piers. 'I'll return at four o'clock to establish how you've lined your ducks up. By focusing your minds, you will achieve the best solutions. When you return to work on Monday, you will have a different outlook on life. Taking time out makes all the difference.'

Sophia took hold of Piers' arm and gave him an in-depth tour of the building; he'd only become acquainted with the West Wing this morning before he sacked the chauffeur. She caught her breath as they stepped into a large room with floor-to-ceiling windows overlooking the gardens. 'This room is my favourite – and it's never used.'

Piers frowned. 'Don't you use it for weddings? Although I must admit, it could do with some work. Where are the weddings held?'

Sophia blushed. 'I can't remember the last time we had a wedding.'

Piers grinned. 'So that was a porky about "a thriving conference and wedding venue"? You naughty girl.'

Sophia sighed. 'You were less than honest too. Why didn't you stop Guy and Nate from stealing your idea about the luxury apartments?'

Piers looked down at her. 'You heard about my

idea?'

'Luca overheard it at lunchtime.'

'Well, I didn't lie. I just didn't own up. There's a time and a place for everything.'

'You are very wise.'

Piers' eyes twinkled as he stroked Sophia's cheek. 'I know.'

A creaking door shattered the "moment". Sophia turned to face Maria. 'Mamma! Why aren't you on Reception?'

Maria squinted up at Piers before turning to whisper to her daughter, 'Is Jessie all right? I didn't see her come back from the pavilion. I hope the ghost of the murdered gardener hasn't frightened her off.'

Sophia whispered back, 'Paris – you remember – Emilio?'

Maria's shoulders softened. 'Oh yes, my memory's escaping me. Carry on with this gentleman. I must get back before I'm missed.'

Piers stared at Sophia. 'Would you like to enlighten me with what's going on?"

6

THE COCKTAIL PARTY

Jessie was impressed with the hotel on the Champs-Elysees. She was surprised Emilio owned a two-bedroom apartment within it. There was an open-plan living room, kitchen, dining area with views of the Eiffel Tower, two bathrooms and a dressing room containing a raft of designer clothes. Jessie let out a low whistle. 'Wow! Your girlfriend's very stylish. I'd love to meet her. What's her name?'

Emilio's eyes shone. 'Claudette.'

Jessie's mouth fell open. 'Your girlfriend's French? Does she live here in Paris?'

Emilio nodded. 'She certainly does. I bought this apartment six months ago so we would have a base whenever I visit France.'

Jessie frowned. 'Doesn't she have her own place?'

Emilio smiled. 'She lives with her parents.'

Jessie raised an eyebrow. She wanted to know more about Claudette – her age, where she worked, what she looked like. But she managed to hold her tongue. Emilio's private life was none of her business.

Emilio opened the door of the spare bedroom to the sight of several dresses displayed on the bed. Jessie gulped before picking one up and turning to her boss. 'You said you'd told your girlfriend my size. These are all far too big. I can't wear any of them without looking like a frump.'

Emilio frowned. 'I said you were the same size as her. The couturier must have got the wrong message.'

Jessie checked the time. 'How long have we got until the cocktail party? If I pop out now, I should be able to pick up a little black dress at a reasonable price. Can I claim it on expenses?'

Emilio shook his head. 'You need to look presentable tonight – only clothes by a top French designer will do.' Emilio paced the room before having a lightbulb moment. 'You can wear one of Claudette's dresses. Choose one from the dressing room and meet me in the living room in an hour. That'll give me time to make a few calls before we go.'

Jessie was annoyed with Claudette. Emilio's girlfriend had deliberately tried to sabotage her evening. Jessie smiled to herself as she made her way through a rail of little black dresses. They were all her size! This felt like a "princess" moment. It helped, too, that Claudette had the same size feet. Jessie chose a mid-length, sleeveless, black dress with side split. She brushed her short blonde hair and was pleased she'd had it cut for the course; it didn't interfere with the back of the dress, which had a large teardrop cutaway design revealing her back and accentuating her tiny waist. Jessie felt a million dollars as she slid her feet into a pair of silver shoes before eyeing up a large selection of bags and choosing one to match.

Now was the time for the finishing touches. Claudette had been underhand, so Jessie had no concern about spraying on her perfume and using her makeup. There was a tray of costume jewellery too. Jessie guessed the most expensive items were locked away in a safe, so she didn't feel guilty about borrowing a pair of diamond earrings and a long diamond chain. The front of the dress was quite plain, and the necklace set it off a treat. Jessie had to admit the "diamonds" were excellent replicas.

When she was ready, Jessie glided into the living room and did a twirl. Emilio's eyes popped. He ended a call and stood up. 'Turn around again.' Jessie did as requested. 'I've never seen Claudette wear that dress. You look amazing. I can't believe you brought diamonds with you to wear on the course. They look great with that dress, though.'

Jessie opened her mouth, and Emilio reached for

his dinner jacket. 'We'd best get a move on. We can't be late.'

*

A waiter offered Jessie a canapé, and she bit into it as she held onto a glass of champagne in her left hand and clutched Claudette's bag under her right arm. She struggled to hold everything and decided to find somewhere to sit down. The bag may have a strap inside she could hang over her shoulder. She'd only opened it earlier to throw in a lipstick, handkerchief, and some money. She hadn't thought about a strap. The hour to get ready wasn't long enough when there was an Aladdin's Cave of designer clothes to choose from.

There was a small table with two chairs near a stage, and Jessie sat down. She placed her glass on the table and opened Claudette's bag. On first inspection, there wasn't a strap inside. Jessie unzipped a pocket in the lining, and her fingers touched a silver chain. That was a relief. Jessie clipped the chain onto the bag and, against her better judgement, opened an envelope folded up in the pocket. She took out a letter and scanned the message:

My Darling Claudette,

I will be in Paris on Wednesday next week. Meet me in my apartment at six o'clock, and we can spend the evening together.

I have another surprise for you – a little something to match your amazing emerald eyes.

Yours as always,

Giuseppe X

Jessie folded the note back up and zipped it inside the handbag. So Claudette was two-timing Emilio. What should Jessie do?

'You're wearing one of my dresses.'

Jessie jumped at the sight of an attractive young man standing before her. The man reached for her hand and kissed it. 'May I ask how you acquired it? I have only given one of that design to my girlfriend, Claudette. The dress will be launched in my latest collection at Paris Fashion Week.'

Jessie's mouth fell open. 'Are you Giuseppe?'

The man shook his head. 'I'm Antoine Chambray.'

Jessie didn't know what to say, so she focused on Claudette. 'I borrowed the dress from Claudette. Have you been going out with her for long?'

'We've been together forever. We met at school. Why did you think I was Giuseppe?'

'Err . . . '

'Ah, let me help you; I do look a little like my best friend. You may have seen him earlier. Unfortunately, Giuseppe couldn't make the cocktail party. He had another appointment tonight from six o'clock.'

Jessie was livid. 'Does Giuseppe have an apartment in Paris?'

'Strange question, but "yes". It's in this very building.'

Jessie's head was spinning as a plan began to fall into place.'

7

REVELATIONS

Back at Hinchingthorpe Manor, Sophia was in a quandary. She didn't want to let her brother down but didn't like lying to Piers either. Sophia had managed to get back to the course this afternoon without divulging anything, but tonight was different. She'd accepted an invitation from Piers to dinner at a nearby restaurant. As Sophia glanced across the table at the very handsome and charming man, she knew she couldn't keep her secret for much longer.

Piers unfolded his serviette. 'Tell me all about yourself. How long have you worked as a trainer at the manor?'

Sophia took a deep breath before responding, 'My brother Luca and I have worked at the manor since we left college, but our mamma, Maria, has been there forever.'

Piers raised an eyebrow. 'It's a real family affair then. How do you know Emilio?'

Sophia lowered her eyes. 'He's our brother.'

Piers spluttered on his wine. 'So that's why Emilio got us all to the Cotswolds on a course. He's ploughing money into your business. Are you and Luca employed by the manor or by a training organisation? Are you qualified in personality profiling? The team could do with some of that if there's time this week.'

Sophia gulped. 'Personality profiling?'

Piers leaned forward and took hold of her hand. 'You and Luca aren't qualified trainers, are you? This whole course is a sham. I need to work out why Emilio's gone to the trouble of neglecting our business to benefit yours.'

Sophia's cheeks reddened. 'I work in housekeeping, and Luca's a chef.'

Piers sat back in his chair as the realisation sank in. 'Everything that happened this morning with the chauffeur was a farce, wasn't it?' Sophia nodded, and Piers let out a sigh. 'But why? Why make a fool of me?'

Sophia chuckled. 'Because Luca said you needed taking down a peg or two. You wanted to be the Lord, so he gave you the role of gardener. It was then up to me to find a reason why the Lady needed a gardener rather than a Lord.'

Piers was stunned and embarrassed. He tried to read the menu while he gathered his thoughts, but that was impossible. He needed to get a matter off his chest. 'Promise you'll never lie to me again.'

Sophia smiled. 'I'm sorry. I'll never lie to you again. What are we having for dinner? The scallops always get good reviews, and the rib-eye steak is best with bearnaise sauce. That's one good thing about having a chef for a brother; Luca's always good with hints and tips where food's concerned.'

Piers was calming down. It wasn't Sophia's fault she'd been put in a compromising position by Emilio. Just wait until he saw his boss again. There was a thought. Sophia had mentioned Emilio, Jessie, and Paris in the same sentence earlier. It was time to test whether she would keep her promise not to lie.

Piers looked up from the menu. 'Why is Jessie in Paris with Emilio?'

Sophia sighed. 'Because Claudette has let him down again. That woman is a bad one. How could she back out of going to a cocktail party at the last minute? The party's in honour of Antoine Chambray, for goodness sake. What I'd give to rub shoulders with a designer like that!'

Piers' eyes were alight as he held his leg out from under the table. 'These shoes are by Antoine. He sent them to me ahead of his show at Paris Fashion Week.'

Sophia gasped. 'You know Antoine Chambray?'

Piers nodded. 'I'm an investor in his business. Thank you for being honest with me. Let's order our food then we can devise a plan to help you and Luca make the most of the next two days. One that doesn't involve me making a fool of myself.'

*

In Paris, Emilio searched for Jessie, who had wandered off and was now sitting near the stage in deep conversation with the Guest of Honour. 'So you're a fashion designer. I'm sorry I didn't realise who you were. My boss hijacked me this afternoon to come here, as his girlfriend couldn't make it.'

Antoine was intrigued by this attractive Englishwoman. She looked better in the dress than Claudette. 'Now let me guess, you're a model.'

Jessie laughed. 'No way! I'm an estate agent. I work for *Rawlinson's Residential* in London.'

Antoine smiled. 'I knew we had a connection. Piers is a good friend of mine; he's helped me buy and sell several properties.'

Emilio stood still to listen to the conversation before raising his eyebrows. Was Piers moonlighting?

Antoine frowned. 'You look amazing in my dress, although I'm very annoyed with Claudette for lending it to you. I'm also shocked she would have the audacity to loan you that necklace and earrings. I gave them to her just last week as a present for our tenth anniversary.'

Emilio took a step backwards. Surely Antoine Chambray wasn't talking about the same Claudette? Jessie reached inside the bag and took out the letter. 'I borrowed Claudette's bag too. You should read this.'

Antoine was surprisingly calm. 'I've had my suspicions that Claudette's been less than faithful for months. I asked Giuseppe Firenzo to help me prove it. He's a good friend, and she's a worthless piece of … of … my time.' Antoine held Jessie's hand in both of his. 'You're a good girl, Jessie. I feel I can trust you. Piers no longer has time to help buy and sell my properties. He's retiring soon. I want to work with *you* in future.'

Jessie gulped. 'I'd be delighted to work with you, Antoine, but only via the correct route. Any properties I help buy and sell for you must go through the books of *Rawlinson's Residential*.'

Emilio grinned as he kept his distance from his rising star performer.

Antoine leaned forward and kissed Jessie on both cheeks. 'It's a deal. But before we sign on the dotted line, I want to give you a gift as a "thank you" present for helping me extract myself from Claudette. You may not accept gifts when we're working together in a professional capacity.'

Jessie smiled. 'OK then if you insist. What gift would you like to give me?'

Antoine pulled Jessie to her feet before twirling her around. 'It would be a crime to take this dress away from you. It's yours. By the way, how did you manage to borrow these things from Claudette when your boss only brought you to Paris this afternoon?'

Emilio stepped forward to shake Antoine's hand. 'I'm Emilio, Head of *Rawlinson's Residential.* I asked my girlfriend to source Jessie's outfit, and she borrowed it from Claudette. It was all very short notice. Anyway, I'm delighted to hear we'll be working with you from now on. Jessie's an excellent agent; you won't be disappointed with your decision. Now, if you'll excuse us, we have another client we need to speak to while we're in Paris.'

Emilio took Jessie by her arm, and she glanced up at him before whispering, 'Wasn't that a bit rude? You cut our conversation short.'

Emilio kept walking. 'What was I supposed to do? I had to think fast. I didn't want to hang around too long in case he asked any more questions. Things will have died down about Claudette before Antoine Chambray requires our services. I can't believe Piers has been working with him directly. No wonder he's thinking of retiring soon.'

Jessie squeezed Emilio's arm. 'Are you upset about Claudette?'

Emilio shook his head. 'She was just a distraction while I'm in Paris. It gets lonely in the evenings when you're away on business. Tables for one are no fun.'

Jessie felt sorry for Emilio; he was putting on a brave face. She tried to lighten the situation. 'That was a fib you told about your girlfriend knowing Claudette. And then you lied again about meeting another client while we're in Paris.' Jessie chuckled. 'I didn't know you had it in you to twist the truth.'

Jessie's hand was linked through Emilio's arm, and he patted it. 'I only twisted the first part.' The pair came to a standstill in front of a tall, distinguished-looking, sandy-haired man. 'Jessie, I want you to meet Logan. He's an old friend of mine; we went to university together.'

Logan held out his hand to shake Jessie's. 'I'm very pleased to meet you, Jessie. Emilio's told me all about you. We'll be seeing a lot of each other in the coming weeks.'

Jessie turned to stare at Emilio, who smiled broadly. 'Logan has the ten-million-pound property we'll shortly be listing. The one I've offered up as a prize on the course.'

Logan raised an eyebrow. 'You're giving away my home on a course?'

Emilio grinned. 'Not exactly. The prize is the commission payment when Jessie sells it.'

Jessie's eyes widened. 'But I haven't been the best delegate on the course – yet. There are still two days to go, and I missed this afternoon.'

Logan smiled. 'Well, you're the only agent I'll work with. I've already made up my mind.'

Emilio winked at Jessie. 'What the client wants, the client gets.'

*

It had been a long evening, and on their way back to Emilio's apartment, Jessie caught sight of herself in a window. 'Oh, my goodness. I should have given Antoine his necklace and earrings back. What am I going to do? I hope he doesn't think I've run off with them.'

Emilio shrugged. 'His mind will be on other things. I just wanted to get out of there. I need to keep a low profile while he finishes things with Claudette.'

Jessie sighed. 'I won't sleep tonight unless I've returned the jewellery. Wait there while I pop back to the cocktail party. I'll find Antoine, give him the necklace and earrings, and say "goodbye" from the both of us.'

Jessie reached the venue for the cocktail party, but the concierge wouldn't let her back in. She stamped her foot. 'I work with Antoine Chambray (well, she would soon), and I have an important item to return to him tonight.'

The concierge held out his hand. 'You could leave the item with me.'

Jessie shook her head as she turned red in the face. 'No! I can't. I must see Antoine tonight.'

The concierge grinned and turned to open the gold-handled glass door for a man to leave the building. 'Good evening, Mr Charteris. Will you return to your apartment tonight, or are you headed for the airport?'

Jessie took a step backwards as a stunned Logan walked towards her. He turned to answer the concierge, 'I was stepping out for some fresh air. I'll be staying in my apartment tonight.' Logan frowned. 'Jessie! I thought you'd left with Emilio.'

Jessie let out a sigh of relief. 'I did. But I need to return something to Antoine Chambray, and I can't get back into the building. Can you help me, please?'

Logan smiled at the concierge. 'Jessie's with me. We'll pop back inside to find Antoine together.'

It didn't take long to find the fashion designer – he was striding through the foyer with a face like thunder. Logan looked down at Jessie and raised his eyebrows. 'Are you sure you want to disturb him while he's in a bad mood?'

Jessie nodded. 'I have to.' She waved an arm in the air. 'Antoine! I need to speak to you.'

Antoine stopped in his tracks. 'Jessie! Is there a

problem?'

Jessie took out the diamond earrings. 'I need to return your jewellery. I'm so sorry, but I forgot I was wearing it until I was walking back to my hotel.'

Jessie tried to unclasp the necklace, but her hands were shaking. Logan noticed her predicament, and he stepped forward. 'Allow me.'

Jessie held her short blonde hair out of the way, and Logan bent down to release the catch. Jessie turned around too soon, and her hair brushed against Logan's face. She felt like a clumsy oaf and wanted to disappear through the floor. Both men were staring at her with grins on their faces. Jessie handed the jewellery to Antoine and made a quick exit. Why couldn't she be composed and elegant like everyone else in Paris? It was lucky Emilio hadn't witnessed *that* embarrassing scene.

8

THURSDAY MORNING

It was almost lunchtime when Jessie wheeled her case through the foyer of Hinchingthorpe Manor. Maria called out to her, 'They're having so much fun on the course today; Piers is an excellent trainer!' Jessie frowned. She wasn't happy in the slightest with Piers. Why had he now taken it upon himself to hijack the course? Jessie already knew she'd won the prize. She just needed to do her best to make it look like the result wasn't a fix.

After dropping her case in her room, Jessie returned to the course to a round of sarcastic applause. Guy was the first to speak, 'The Lady has returned. Rumour has it you popped over to France for a cocktail party. Well, we have to admit you're taking the role very seriously. That's just the sort of thing a Lady would do.' There were sniggers around the room. Everyone knew

Jessie had skived off. They just wished they had her nerve.

Jessie sat in her seat in the front row and glared at Piers, who was drawing on a whiteboard. He turned around and smiled at her. 'We've been busy in your absence, Jessie. We're contemplating what life's about. Do we want to be estate agents forever? Can we do better things than work our butts off around the clock to bring in the commission? Do we want to be working for Emilio, who reaps in the rewards of our endeavours?'

Jessie stood up and turned to face the team. 'We should also consider if it's wise to undercut the business by working with clients directly. Some of you may have considered doing so but will have decided against it. *Rawlinson's Residential* prides itself on ethical behaviour. There's a wealth of business out there if we work together to bring it in. Surely it's best not to line our pockets at the expense of our colleagues?'

Nate leaned back in his chair. 'Wait a minute. Where's all of this going? What *were* you up to last night?'

Jessie ran a hand through her short blonde hair. 'I was on a mission to bring in international business to benefit us all. I know I wasn't supposed to be working, but this opportunity was too good to miss. The fashion designer Antoine Chambray has a whole portfolio of properties worldwide, and he wants to work with us.'

There were gasps around the room before Jessie received admiring smiles and nods. Guy lifted his phone and Googled Antoine Chambray. 'Oh, my God! There's an image of Jessie with Antoine Chambray in Paris last night.'

Everyone else Googled away, and Nate handed Jessie her phone. He noticed her shocked expression. 'Piers arranged for us all to have our phones back, so I looked after yours for you. We've been able to keep on top of a few things. You're not the only one working over the last twenty-four hours.'

Jessie was livid, and she turned to face Piers. 'You do realise this course has become a shambles because of you? What did you all do yesterday afternoon? Did the lottery winners come up with any good ideas for the manor? Did you even try to be a gardener to make a difference for the Lady?'

The door to the meeting room opened, and Emilio walked in. 'I should have known my enthusiastic team wouldn't be able to leave work behind for three days. I'm calling an end to the course now. You can stay here and catch up with emails or head back to London immediately.'

Emilio placed an arm around Piers' shoulders. 'I've heard about your great idea for this place. I'm not surprised it was you who came up with the goods. We'll have buyers waiting to snap the manor up with your luxury apartment solution.'

Piers rubbed his chin. 'When's the property coming onto the market?'

'As soon as we want it to. The owners have left the sale in my capable hands.'

Piers stared at his boss. 'We need to have a private discussion.'

Jessie's phone flashed up with a message. She took a deep breath before holding her hand in the air. 'We all need to stay at the manor for the rest of the week. It will take the whole team to deal with this.' Emilio raised his eyebrows, and Jessie continued, 'Antoine is arriving here tomorrow with Giuseppe. He says they both have properties for us to sell.'

Piers enlightened the rest of the team. 'I'm well acquainted with Antoine Chambray. I invested in the start-up of his business.' Piers lowered his eyes. 'I've also given him some advice regarding real estate over the years.' Piers cleared his throat before continuing, 'His close friend Giuseppe Firenzo is a prominent jewellery designer. Both men have significant property portfolios. I'll facilitate an introduction for you guys.' Piers' eyes sparkled. 'I would never have thought it, but this course has made me realise what I need at this stage of my life.'

Guy snorted. 'What's that?'

Piers didn't hesitate to respond, 'A Lady of the Manor.'

Guy nudged Nate. 'He's after Jessie. She'll become rich if she marries him.'

Emilio overheard the conversation, and he confronted Guy. 'Jessie's already rich. She's her own woman with great morals, who'll go far in the real estate business.'

Nate stared at Emilio. 'But is that enough? Doesn't everyone want a soul mate? Someone to go to dinner with; watch TV with in the evening? This job can be quite lonely, especially if we're going to be travelling around the world.'

Emilio stared at Jessie before responding, 'You're right, Nate. Jessie deserves so much more. I'm beginning to think this course has had some impact. You're all thinking about what matters in life. I must admit that taking just a fraction of time out yesterday has impacted me too.'

Guy asked the million-dollar question, 'So who will win the ten-million-pound listing? None of us would have turned up if you hadn't dangled that carrot.'

Emilio didn't take his eyes off Jessie. He could still see her in that little black dress dripping with diamonds. As far as Claudette was concerned, she was history. His French fling wasn't a patch on Jessie.

Guy interrupted Emilio's thoughts. 'So, what's the answer?'

Emilio's phone flashed, and he read the message before relaying it to the rest of the team, 'The owner of the ten-million-pound property will also be coming here tomorrow. A prize can't be awarded because we failed to complete the course. I'll leave it to the client to choose which agent he wants to work with.'

Guy scoffed. 'I bet it's Jessie. She's on a winning streak.'

9

BACK TO WORK

It was business as usual for the rest of the day. The team set up their laptops in the conference room and tried to clear the way for the influx of new opportunities.

Word had spread that Emilio had coerced the team to the Cotswolds on false pretences. He was just after ideas to save the manor from disrepair. His ulterior motive had been to protect the jobs of his immediate family. However, in a roundabout way, by taking a day or two away from their jobs, the team at *Rawlinson's Residential* were revitalised and ready for action.

What Emilio hadn't allowed for, was the mind-blowing chain of events over the last twenty-four hours that had left him questioning where his own life was leading. By the end of the afternoon, he found himself sharing confidences with Piers in the hotel's bar.

Piers began the questioning, 'How old are you, Emilio?'

'Thirty-two.'

'Well, I'm thirty-nine. It's taken until now for me to realise there's more to life than work.'

Emilio raised an eyebrow. 'I'd say your enlightenment has come at a point where you're so loaded you don't need to work. If you hadn't already advised me of your intention to retire, I would have been forced to take disciplinary action against you. You've reaped in a fortune over the years with deals you haven't put through our books.'

Piers lowered his head, and Emilio continued, 'What will you do when you retire? You're already well-travelled. Are you thinking of buying a yacht? A football team? A racehorse?'

Piers shook his head. 'None of those. I want to buy this place – ghosts and all. I've been thinking about my luxury apartment idea, and I've come up with a better one.'

Emilio raised an eyebrow. 'What's that?'

'I'm going to live here. It's an excellent place to

bring up a family.'

There it was! Emilio had been right all along. Hinchingthorpe Manor suited Piers to the ground. He could Lord around in a place like this for fifty years. Emilio grinned at the thought of lots of little Piers' running around playing cricket. He also felt great satisfaction that his family's jobs would be saved. Piers would need a chef and a housekeeper. His mother's job may be at risk, though. A family home wouldn't need a receptionist. That bothered Emilio. 'What about my mamma? Would she still have a part to play? She's worked here for as long as I can remember. It would break her heart if she had to leave.'

Piers' eyes twinkled. 'Don't worry; your mother won't be a deal breaker. Maria can live here as long as she wants. She'll have a luxury apartment. A type of Granny Annex.'

Realisation hit Emilio like a bolt of lightning. Piers had a soft spot for Sophia. He had everything planned out! Piers always got what he set out to achieve. If this master plan came off, Piers would become Emilio's brother-in-law. Emilio had to admit that wouldn't be such a bad thing. He wished *he* had the vision and drive to sort out *his* life.

Emilio's phone rang, and he took the call. 'Logan! What time will you be arriving in the morning? You'll never believe it, but Antoine Chambray and his friend will be coming here tomorrow too. We'll have an extra busy day. What do you mean you're outside? You're here to take Jessie out to dinner? No! No … that's no problem at all. Does Jessie know? I see … you've just spoken with her. I could always join you. What do you mean there's no room at the restaurant?'

Piers grabbed Emilio's arm and shook his head as he whispered, 'End the call.'

Emilio rubbed his forehead. 'Well, have a good time tonight. I'll see you in the morning.'

Piers spoke softly, 'I'm well on the way to getting the girl of my dreams. Who wouldn't want to be Lady of the Manor?' He locked eyes with Emilio and was relieved his boss had interpreted his plans without animosity. 'I'll help you win Jessie's heart. Just leave it to me.'

*

All Jessie wanted was an early night. It was unfortunate Logan had arrived earlier than anticipated. She'd suggested he had dinner with his old friend Emilio, but Logan was having none of it. He said there was no time to waste now they were working together on selling his ten-million-pound property. Jessie felt very uncomfortable; there was no way the rest of the team would accept her "winning the prize", particularly when Antoine and Giuseppe turned up in the morning and wanted her to work with them too. It was no fun being popular. Jessie had an idea . . .

*

Logan was greeted in Reception by Guy and Nate. Guy held out his hand. 'Hi, it's Logan, isn't it? Unfortunately, Jessie's running late, so she's sent us to buy you a drink in the bar. She'll be down when she's finished her conference call.'

The men wandered into the bar area, and Emilio rose to his feet. 'Logan! Where's Jessie?'

Guy winked at Emilio without Logan noticing. 'She's on a conference call. We're buying Logan a drink while he's waiting.'

Piers stood up to shake hands with the new client. 'I'm Piers. It's very good to meet you, Logan. I'll join you all if I may. Emilio needs to dash off.' Piers gave Emilio a shove, and he headed for the conference room. He was pleased Jessie was keeping Logan waiting. However, the conference room was locked. Emilio phoned Jessie.

'Oh, hi Emilio. I'm in my room. I've been very naughty. After last night I fancied a night in with a room service meal. I sent Guy and Nate to look after Logan. After a few drinks, Logan won't notice I'm missing. I know I've been unprofessional, but I hope you forgive me.'

Emilio's heart flew. 'Of course, I forgive you. I'd rather have a night in too. Have you ordered your food yet?'

'Not yet.'

'Do you mind if I join you?'

Jessie caught her breath. 'Of course not.'

'Well, I'm on my way then.'

Emilio turned to see Piers holding a bottle of champagne and two glasses. 'With my compliments. I suggest you steer clear of garlic tonight.'

Emilio's smile lit up the murky corridor. 'You're a good friend, Piers.'

Piers slapped Emilio on the back. 'I know.'

10

A CUNNING PLAN

Emilio bounded into the conference room the following morning to discover Piers had beaten him to it. 'You're early, Piers. Everyone's still in the restaurant having breakfast. Logan looks a bit worse for wear. I managed to avoid him, so he didn't ask me any questions about Jessie.'

Piers grinned. 'How did it go last night? Did the champagne work its magic?'

Emilio blushed. 'We had a nice evening, thanks. It was very pleasant.'

Piers pushed for further information. 'Don't tell me things are still on a platonic basis. You're a bit backward in coming forward. Last night was your big chance.'

Emilio changed the subject. 'It's a big day today. We need to keep the focus on work.'

Piers was no fool. Emilio was wearing the same shirt and socks as yesterday. He also smelt of flowery deodorant. Piers knew just the right thing to say to wind up his boss, 'You do realise that Logan, Antoine, and Giuseppe will be fighting over Jessie today. How will you motivate the rest of the team when she's become your star player overnight?'

That thought hadn't escaped Emilio. He'd been wrestling with what to do. 'I have an idea. Just leave it with me.'

Emilio headed for the Reception to speak with his mother. 'Mamma, I need to borrow your ring.'

Maria threw her hands in the air. 'You're too late! Sophia's already taken it from me. What on earth is going on with you two?!'

Emilio turned on his heels in search of his sister. Sophia was in the laundry room singing along to a song on the radio. He needed to act quickly, or his plan for today would be scuppered. 'I need to borrow mamma's ring; she says you have it.'

Sophia nodded. 'That's right. Mamma's ring will go to me when I get married.'

Emilio sighed and held his sister's shoulders.

'Look, I know I shouldn't interfere in your personal life but trust me, Piers will buy you a much better ring when he proposes. I need to borrow mamma's ring now, or I'll have a mutiny on my hands today with the team.'

Sophia burst out laughing. 'If you weren't my brother, I'd think you'd lost the plot. I need the ring to give to Gino. He's coming over from Italy at the weekend to get down on one knee.'

'Gino?'

'My boyfriend, Gino.'

'I didn't know you had a boyfriend.'

Sophia shrugged her shoulders. 'That's not my problem.'

Emilio rubbed his face with both hands. This whole team event was turning into a disaster. All he'd wanted was to save his family's jobs by Piers buying a haunted house that no one else would touch. There were already raised eyes in the team about Emilio whisking Jessie away to Paris when everyone else had been lured to the course on false pretences. If Logan insisted on Jessie being the agent for his ten-million-pound listing, they would be up in arms. With Sophia's news, Piers wouldn't buy the manor, and everything would return to square one. Emilio was at his wits' end.

Sophia felt her brother's angst. 'How long do you need the ring for?'

Emilio's muddled thoughts were broken. 'Just today.'

Sophia reached for her handbag and removed a handkerchief containing a small sapphire ring. She handed the ring to Emilio. 'Don't lose it. You have until the morning to give it back.'

Emilio felt a glimmer of hope. He could still turn things around. He kissed his sister and went in search of Jessie.

Jessie was having breakfast with Guy and Nate in the dining room. Emilio strode up to them. 'I need a word with you, Jessie. Join me outside on the terrace as soon as you can.'

Guy winked at Nate, who raised his eyebrows. Jessie gulped down her coffee. 'Sorry, boys. The boss has summoned me.' Jessie placed her serviette on the table before standing up. 'I'll see you both in the conference room. It's a big day for us all today.'

Jessie opened a door onto the terrace where Emilio was waiting for her. She blushed as she smiled at him. 'We had a great time last night, didn't we?'

Emilio's eyes twinkled. 'We had the best time ever. I don't have time to explain in detail, but I need you to pretend you're engaged.'

Jessie gulped. 'Engaged?!'

Emilio took the ring out of his pocket and showed it to her. 'This is my mother's ring. I borrowed it for today. It will protect you from the advances of Antoine, Giuseppe, and Logan. If they think you're engaged, they'll leave you alone, and I'll be able to share their properties around the team without anyone making a fuss.'

Jessie giggled. 'Who am I supposed to be engaged to?'

Emilio shuffled his feet. 'I don't know. You don't need to give any details. Just say your fiancé's based in Dubai or something. They may not ask questions. Hopefully, they won't go near you when they see the ring.' Emilio locked eyes with Jessie. 'Please, will you do this for me? I promise it will turn out for the best in the end.'

Jessie nodded and held her hand out while Emilio slid the ring into place.

Guy thumped Nate. 'Did you see that?'

Nate's eyes were on stalks. 'I certainly did!'

Emilio's mind was racing. Thankfully Jessie was on board with his plan to spread the influx of business around the team. It would mean less commission for her, but she was realistic. She'd never be able to cope with all the new clients who'd emerged overnight. He knew he could trust Jessie to the point where he'd confided in her last night about Piers' intentions with Sophia.

Jessie glanced at her phone. 'We'd best get a move on. I'll flash your mother's ring at Logan first, and then he can decide which other agent he wants to work with. That sounds like a good place to start.'

Emilio flung an arm around Jessie's shoulders. 'You're a star; thanks for helping me out of this hole.'

Jessie smiled up at him. 'I'm up for doing anything that keeps the team happy. Happy team, happy boss.'

Emilio's eyes shone. 'Let's get through today; then there's another issue I need your advice on.'

Jessie raised an eyebrow. 'Can you give me a clue?'

Emilio frowned. 'Sophia's getting engaged at the weekend to her boyfriend – someone called Gino – I've never met him. I need to give her mamma's ring back before we leave. Sophia will give it to Gino so he can use it when he proposes.'

Jessie's jaw dropped as she twisted the sapphire ring on her finger. 'But you said last night that Piers has his sights set on Sophia, and he's planning on buying the manor to use as their family home.'

Emilio sighed. 'I know. What a mess! You and I must be creative to salvage the situation in my family's best interests.' Emilio winked at Jessie. 'For a start, Sophia's never liked sapphires, and Piers wouldn't propose with a second-hand ring.'

11

MAMMA'S RING

Logan was in the conference room chatting with Piers when Emilio and Jessie arrived. Emilio slapped him on the shoulder. 'You're keen. I know you've only met Jessie and a couple of other agents so far, but it's your lucky day today – the whole team's here, and it's up to you to choose the best fit for you.'

Logan frowned, and Jessie bit her nail on her left hand while trying to manoeuvre the sapphire to get a glint from the ceiling lights. If biting her nails didn't turn Logan off, an engagement ring would focus his mind on a different agent. Logan stared at her. 'Is that an engagement ring you're wearing?'

Jessie smiled and nodded while she thought of what to say. 'I'm so happy!'

Logan held his hand out to shake hers. 'Congratulations. When are you getting married?'

Jessie looked to the floor. 'Hopefully, next year. We're both so busy at the moment.'

Logan nodded. 'I know what it's like. I'm marrying the love of my life next week. Not getting my house on the market sooner has been a real pain. I must do a deal with you guys today, or Fiona will divorce me before we've even signed on the dotted line.'

Jessie stopped biting her nail, and Emilio stared at her before his shoulders shook with a mixture of surprise and relief. Logan frowned at his friend. 'What's so funny?'

Emilio composed himself and held out his hand to shake Logan's. 'Congratulations, old man! I'm surprised, that's all. My invite must have got lost in the post.'

Logan blushed. 'We've not sent any invites. We're eloping to Gretna Green: family feuds and all that. I'd have married Fiona years ago if our relatives hadn't done their best to keep us apart. Time's moving on now, though. I'm thirty-two and finally taking control of my life.'

Emilio felt sad for his friend. 'Don't worry. We're the best team to sell your property. Jessie's up to her eyes in it at the moment with listings. I want you to get a one-to-one service, and I'm recommending Nate as your agent.' Emilio held a finger to his lips before speaking, 'As you know, I've offered your business as an incentive to the team. I know you like Jessie; everyone does, but Nate is your best fit.'

Logan rubbed his chin. 'I'd rather work with Guy. He's an expert on Scotch whisky.'

Jessie suppressed a giggle as Emilio devised a plan. 'Logan, we've been friends for years. I need your help. After you've met all of my agents today and, if it's still Guy you want to work with on selling your property, I'll make sure it happens. I need to be fair to my team and give them all a chance with opportunities like this.'

Logan ushered Emilio into the corridor before lowering his voice, 'You've always been fair, Emilio. It would help if you put yourself first for a change. Logan winked at his friend before whispering, 'Jessie's a great woman. You should snap her up.'

Emilio's heart was pounding. 'But … but … she's engaged.'

Logan slapped Emilio on the back. 'I don't know what the pair of you are playing at, but I can tell when you're lying. Jessie's even worse than you at faking it!'

Emilio took a step backwards before answering his phone. 'Antoine and Giuseppe are here. I need to meet them in Reception.'

*

All team members were in place when Emilio returned to the conference room with his guests. He introduced everyone before standing at the front of the room to make a presentation on the services the *Rawlinson's Residential* team could offer their clients. Logan, Antoine, and Giuseppe were all seated in the front row, and when Antoine turned round to smile at Jessie, she waved with her left hand and then fiddled with the ring so that he couldn't miss it. She had to admit the sapphire was too small for her liking, but Antoine turned around a few times to stare at it. Job done! He knew she was engaged and could choose another agent to work with.

Jessie was beginning to wonder how *she* would benefit from all of this. If Emilio gave away listings to her colleagues, surely he should include her too? From being in demand, Jessie was starting to feel left out. She didn't worry for too long. Seeing Emilio standing tall at the front of the room, with his sleek black hair and shiny brown eyes, her stomach flipped. This devastatingly handsome man had taken her to a cocktail party in Paris, then spent the night with her in a haunted house – it wasn't *her* fault she was scared when her bedroom window kept rattling.

On top of that, Emilio had confided in her about Piers' plans and now wanted her help with his family's predicament. Emilio had always kept himself detached from the team, so Jessie felt special with his sudden interest in her. All thoughts of fighting for high-level commission listings couldn't be further from her mind.

During the mid-morning coffee break, Antoine made a beeline for Jessie. 'Let me have a closer look at that ring.'

Jessie smiled as she held out her hand. Questions would come next about her engagement. They didn't. Antoine asked Jessie to remove the ring, and he scrutinised it before calling Giuseppe over. 'Am I right in thinking this is a Leopaulo Constantini?'

Giuseppe's eyes widened as he viewed the ring through a magnifying glass. 'It certainly is.' Giuseppe turned his attention to Jessie. 'Has it been in your family for long?'

Jessie opened her mouth, but a grinning Guy spoke first as he poked her in the back. 'Emilio gave it to her this morning – they're engaged.'

There were gasps around the room as the news swept through it, Emilio had no choice but to put the matter straight in the best way he could think of, 'Don't go starting rumours. I only gave Jessie my mamma's ring to look after for the day. She .. she … asked me to get it cleaned.'

Antoine frowned. 'This ring shouldn't be worn. It should be in a safe.'

Giuseppe nodded as he handed the ring to Emilio. 'Antoine is correct.'

Emilio glanced at Jessie as he felt the ring burning his palm. 'Well, I'll put it in a safe now and give your kind advice to my mamma. I won't be long. As soon as I'm back, we can discuss your property portfolios and agree which agents you'll work with.'

Logan crept behind Emilio down the dark corridor before tapping him on the shoulder. Emilio jumped. 'You scared the life out of me.'

Logan chuckled. 'I told you Jessie wasn't engaged. I don't know what you're both playing at with that ring, but I'm intrigued to find out.'

Emilio sighed. 'Mamma's given the ring to Sophia. Her boyfriend's coming over from Italy tomorrow to propose to her.'

Logan raised his eyebrows. 'Is that so? Is he coming over for your sister's hand in marriage or the ring from your mother's finger?'

Emilio turned white, and Logan patted him on the back. 'Get the ring in a safe and count your lucky stars that Jessie's allure attracted Antoine and Giuseppe over here today, or you wouldn't know your family's been sitting on a fortune.'

Emilio nodded before hurrying off, and Logan

allowed himself a cheeky grin. He'd worked out what Emilio was up to. His friend had asked Jessie to pretend she was engaged so that today's affluent clients, including himself, would keep their distance. Emilio *had* got it bad!

12

TIME TO BREATHE

With the clients and team from *Rawlinson's Residential* on their way home for the weekend, Emilio had time to breathe. He'd asked Jessie to stay an extra night to help him with his family predicament. The last few days had been stressful, and dinner with Jessie in a quaint local restaurant was just what he needed.

Emilio clinked wine glasses with Jessie, and she beamed from ear to ear. 'I can't believe how it all turned out today. Logan's happy to work with Guy on his ten-million-pound listing in Scotland and Nate's managing Antoine's property portfolio in the UK.'

Emilio's brown eyes shone as he smiled at Jessie. 'That just leaves Giuseppe.'

Jessie gave a little clap. 'I know! I can't believe you talked him into working directly with you! He would never have given us his palazzo in Rome to sell otherwise. He was so near to doing a deal with an agency in Italy.'

Emilio didn't take his eyes off Jessie as he sipped his wine. 'I'll need you to work with me on such a lucrative listing. I'm flying to Rome next week and will take you with me. I'll lead the project, but you'll be the main agent. Your commission payment will reflect your workload.'

Jessie couldn't believe her luck as she tried to contain her excitement. 'Of course, that's no problem.' Jessie's attention was drawn to the window; a gale was blowing outside. 'I hope my windows aren't rattling again tonight. The manor is so spooky at times. Do you know any ghost stories you can tell me while we're in the safety of this restaurant?'

Emilio laughed. 'I've not heard of one single confirmed sighting of a ghost at Hinchingthorpe Manor. People are great at starting rumours. Unfortunately, gossip like that sticks.'

Jessie frowned. 'Has your mother never told you about the ghost of the murdered gardener that haunts the cricket pavilion? She looked quite scared when she told me about it.'

Emilio raised his eyes. 'Many times. It's the most bizarre thing I've ever heard. My mamma must be getting paid to spook the guests. I can think of no other reason why she would tell such a tale.'

Jessie raised her eyebrows before tapping her bare ring finger. 'Speaking of your mother . . .'

Emilio sat back in his chair. 'Now that's a concern. I can't believe mamma's been walking around with a fortune on her finger for most of her life. What should I do about tomorrow? There's a good chance this "Gino" is coming for the ring, not Sophia's hand in marriage.'

There was a screech from a table in a shady alcove, and Jessie grabbed Emilio's hand. 'Maybe this place is haunted too!'

They both turned to see a shiny black shoe poking out from the darkness before another black shoe followed it and then the whole of Piers stood up. Jessie gasped as Piers walked towards their table, before bending down to whisper, 'You two should keep your voices down. It's a good job it's quiet in here tonight. I'm two steps ahead of the game, as usual. I know how your mother obtained the ring, *and* I will stop any whiff of a proposal from Gino to Sophia. Just watch this space.'

*

Back at the manor, Emilio went in search of his mother. 'Where did you get the ring that's now locked in the safe?'

Maria lowered her eyes. 'I found it in Lost Property when I started working here. How was I to know it was valuable?'

Emilio cringed. 'Have you been making up stories about ghosts?'

Maria was offended. 'I never make up stories.'

Emilio sighed. 'Well, I suggest you stop mentioning ghosts until we get a buyer for the manor. I brought my team here this week, knowing that one of my agents would fall in love with this place and want to turn it into a family home. I had everything lined up until Sophia dropped a bombshell.'

'What bombshell?'

'That her boyfriend's coming over from Italy tomorrow to propose.'

'Oh, that. Well, he'll have to ask me for Sophia's hand in marriage first, and I won't be giving it to him.'

Emilio frowned. 'Why not?'

'Because I've given it to someone else.'

Emilio rubbed his forehead; this whole situation

was becoming exhausting. 'May I ask who you've given it to?'

'That nice young man with a Porsche. He's promised me a Granny Annex.'

Sophia was lurking in the shadows. Her heart sank. How could her mamma use her daughter to manipulate things to her advantage? She felt trapped. As Sophia headed back to her room, she came up with a bright idea; she'd stop Gino from coming here tomorrow and go to Rome to be with him. Her fingers touched on the ring inside her pocket – she'd been annoyed Emilio had put it in the safe without telling her – it was lucky she'd seen him do it. Now she knew her mamma's ring was valuable; she'd take it to Italy. Gino was a well-established businessman, but they could sell it if they ever needed the money. Her mamma had always promised it to her, and promises should be kept.

13

WHERE'S SOPHIA?

The following morning, Piers walked through the dining room with a spring in his step. He was confident Hinchingthorpe Manor would make an excellent family home. Piers wouldn't rush things with Sophia; he'd buy the house and take his time to win her heart. He knew there was a spark there. Why else would they have had a "moment" when she'd given him a tour of the place?

Maria's fingers ran over a number on a piece of paper Piers had given her. She had a job to do; Piers had asked her to call him as soon as Gino entered the building. Goodness knows how Piers would turn this mess around. Daughters could be so troublesome at times.

*

Sophia climbed into a taxi at Rome airport. Her heart was beating fast. Deep down, she had a sinking feeling. Gino hadn't been pleased when she said she was coming to see him. He'd been more concerned about the ring than her. She was also disappointed he hadn't offered to pick her up at the airport. Sophia sensed she was making a big mistake, but she wasn't one to admit such a thing. When her mind was made up, no one would ever change it. Sophia had left the leafy Cotswolds behind for the excitement of Rome!

*

By lunchtime, Maria was becoming concerned. She hadn't seen Sophia all morning, and that was very unusual. Sophia was always roaming around the manor, even on her days off. It wasn't just a place of work for Sophia – it was her home. She tidied the shabby cushions and mats in the foyer as if they were her own. Maria smiled to herself; with her daughter's commitment to making the best of what the manor had to offer, she was keeping it alive.

Maria phoned Sophia's room again – still no answer. With Luca busy in the kitchen, Maria called Emilio, 'It's Mamma. I can't leave Reception. I'm worried about Sophia; I haven't seen her today.'

Emilio rubbed his chin as he raised his eyebrows at Jessie and Piers. 'Don't worry, Mamma. I'll pop along to her room; she'll be getting ready before her boyfriend arrives.'

Maria put the phone down and smiled at a guest who the chauffeur had just collected from the station. After Maria had checked the new arrival into the manor, a porter took hold of the man's bags and led him to his room. Maria's eyes were quite bad, and she was in a frenzy about the whole Sophia situation. She called over to the chauffeur, 'Charles! Will you check something for me?'

When Charles was close enough, Maria lowered her voice, 'Does the signature here resemble the name "Gino"? It doesn't look like it to me.'

Charles put his glasses on. 'It says "Roger Smythe".'

Maria let out a sigh. 'That's a relief. He's far too old for my Sophia. I wonder when Gino's going to arrive. I'm tied to Reception until he turns up, and it's lunchtime now. I'm getting too old not to take a break.'

Charles handed his glasses to Maria. 'Have a look in the diary for last night. I wrote the booking in there myself.'

Maria wore the glasses and was amazed at how well she could see. She opened the diary entitled "Chauffeur Bookings" and read the entry out loud:

> *7.00 pm - Take Miss Sophia to airport hotel. (Note for Maria: She's flying to Rome early in the morning to meet with someone called Gino.)*

Maria threw a hand to her mouth as Charles held *his* hand out for the return of his glasses. 'I wrote the note for you as it all seemed a bit "hush-hush". Sophia was chatting to someone called "Gino" while she was in the car – he was very keen that she'd got "the ring". I thought you should know what's going on. If *I* had a daughter who'd done a "runner", I'd want someone to tell *me*.'

Maria rushed from Reception to the bar area, just as Emilio strode back in. Piers and Jessie were sitting at a table working on their laptops. Emilio was out of breath. 'I've checked her room, and she's not there.'

Maria waved her arms in the air. 'Sophia's in Rome, and she's taken the ring with her!'

Jessie's phone vibrated, and she read a message. Her face turned white. Emilio stared at her. 'Who's the message from?'

Jessie placed her phone on the table. 'Sophia – but she's asked me not to tell anyone.'

Maria's eyes were on stalks. 'Is she engaged yet?'

Jessie sighed. 'Now I'm in a difficult position;

what should I do?'

Piers leaned back in his chair. 'You should go to Rome. It's great that Sophia feels comfortable confiding in you.'

Emilio started checking flights on his phone. 'We'll go together. We need to be there next week anyway.'

Piers shook his head. 'It's best that Jessie goes on ahead. We must ensure Sophia has the best advice and support at this critical time. Jessie needs to get there before anything happens to your sister.'

Maria wrung her hands together. 'Or the ring.'

Emilio scratched his head. 'There are seats available on the late afternoon flight. We'll get you to the airport on time if we leave now.'

Maria headed back to Reception, and Jessie went to pack her bag. Piers smiled at a deflated-looking Emilio. 'Your time will come. You need to take a back seat for now. Let Jessie fly freely. She'll land where she's meant to be.'

14

WELCOME TO ROME

Jessie landed in Rome on Saturday evening. She was met at the airport by Sophia with an appreciative hug. 'You didn't have to come all this way to help me out of a predicament, but I'm delighted you did. I've booked you into the same hotel as me. We'll drop off your bag, then hit the town!'

Jessie glanced around. 'Is Gino with you?'

Sophia shook her head. 'He's history. Can you believe Gino didn't bother to meet me at the airport? He didn't want me to stay in his apartment either. The final straw came when I said I'd lost mamma's ring on the way here. You should have seen his face! I'm not sure which one of us ended it at that point. All I know is I could do with a drink.'

Jessie's face dropped. 'I'm so sorry about Gino,

Sophia. Did you really lose the ring?'

Sophia giggled before waving her left hand in the air. 'Of course not! I just needed to prove that Gino wanted the ring more than me. I had my suspicions.'

Jessie gulped. 'Should you be wearing the ring now? What if we bump into Gino – or one of his friends?'

Sophia sighed as she slipped the ring from her finger. 'You're right. *You* should wear it for safekeeping.'

Jessie wheeled her case to the taxi rank while Sophia clung onto her spare arm. Jessie glanced at Emilio's sister. 'Where are we going tonight? I'm short of clothes. I have nothing special to wear except a dress Antoine Chambray gave me in Paris on Wednesday night.'

Sophia squeezed Jessie's arm. 'Ooooh! Listen to you – Paris on Wednesday, Rome on Saturday. You're really living the high life working for my brother.' Jessie smiled to herself. It *had* been quite a week! Sophia continued, 'Well, I needed some retail therapy this afternoon, so I went out and bought two dresses. We can't let the side down.'

'What side?'

'British girls on the loose in Rome.'

*

Sophia was ready first, and she knocked on Jessie's door with a bottle of wine and two glasses. 'Wow! You look amazing in that dress. Pale blue matches your eyes.' Sophia did a twirl. 'What do you think of mine?'

'You look fantastic! Baby pink goes great with your raven hair. Thanks so much for buying me a dress. Let me know how much I owe you.'

Sophia waved an arm in the air. 'There's no charge. Emilio's paying our expenses this weekend. He messaged me to make sure I keep you safe.'

Jessie lowered her eyes. 'Are you annoyed with me for telling Emilio where you are?'

Sophia smiled. 'I'm not surprised; you two are as thick as thieves. I'm sorry for asking you to keep things quiet. I just wanted time to clear my head and make the right decision. In the end, the decision was taken from me.' Sophia pointed to Jessie's hand. 'That ring was more valuable to Gino than the chance of a lifetime with me.'

Jessie twisted the ring. 'Well, Gino is an idiot. We should put the ring in the hotel safe before we go out.'

Sophia poured the wine and handed a glass to Jessie. 'Let's do a "cheers".'

Jessie suddenly felt exhausted. Sophia wasn't in

any trauma; coming to Rome earlier than planned had been a waste of time. She lifted her glass. 'What are we "cheering" about?'

'That I'm not going to become Signora Constantini. I want a man who loves *me*, not a piece of jewellery.'

Jessie clinked glasses with Sophia before choking on her wine. 'Did you say "Constantini"?'

Sophia's eyes widened. 'Yes. Why?'

Jessie's fatigue had lifted, and she was on red alert as she held out her hand. 'Because this ring is a Leopaulo Constantini. How did you meet Gino?'

'He came to stay at the manor a month ago.' Sophia's memory came flooding back. 'I should have known then he was after the ring!'

'Tell me what happened?'

'He saw mamma wearing it and questioned me about how she got it. I said she'd had it for as long as I could remember and that it would be mine when I married.'

Jessie sighed. 'Didn't you think it was a bit quick that he was coming over again this weekend to propose?'

Sophia blushed. 'Now I think of it – of course.

Italians can be very charming, though, and I've always wanted a "love at first sight" happy ending.'

'Surely you weren't in love with him?'

'No, I wasn't. I was just "in love" with the idea of getting married and starting a family. Gino wants six children.'

Jessie reached for her phone, and Sophia frowned. 'Who are you calling?'

'Giuseppe. He'll be aware of Gino Constantino. We need protection while we're over here.'

*

Thirty minutes later, the girls met with tall, dark-haired, olive-skinned Giuseppe in their hotel bar. He kissed them on both cheeks and flashed a white smile that lit up his handsome face. Jessie drew a deep breath. Claudette must be a beauty to attract Antoine, Giuseppe, *and* Emilio. She composed herself as she articulated the story of the ring, Gino, and the abandoned proposal to *Rawlinson Residential's* latest client.

Giuseppe sat back in his chair as his brown eyes twinkled. 'So, you beautiful signorinas require my help. The first question I would ask is: Why didn't Gino Constantino say that the ring belonged to his family, and he wanted it back?'

Jessie and Sophia sat forward in their chairs. 'Why?'

'Because the ring no longer belongs to his family.'

Jessie rubbed her forehead, and Giuseppe smiled. 'Don't do that. Your face is too pretty for lines.'

Sophia kicked Jessie under the table before winking at her. Jessie wanted to solve the current problem, rather than create another one by attracting a client's attention. She placed her hands in her lap before asking Giuseppe for advice, 'What would you suggest Sophia's family does with the ring?'

Giuseppe reached out to hold Jessie's hand to examine the ring. She slid it off her finger and gave it to him. Giuseppe closed his palm around it before leaning forward and lowering his voice, 'Firstly, I will lock it in the safe at my palazzo. Secondly, I will have it valued if that's what you wish. Thirdly, you should sell it at auction.'

Sophia had questions: 'Firstly, is the ring my mamma's to sell? She found it in Lost Property over forty years ago. Secondly, wouldn't it be nice for it to go back to Gino's family? Thirdly, how can we trust you?'

Jessie gulped. 'Of course, we can trust Giuseppe; he's a famous jewellery designer and one of our prominent clients.'

Giuseppe smiled at Sophia. 'You are quite right to ask questions, signorina. My answers are as follows: Firstly, after so long on your mamma's finger with no one claiming it – the ring is hers. Secondly, if Gino's family want it, they should pay for it. Thirdly, you are right not to trust a man you've just met.'

Giuseppe stood up. 'I will go back to my palazzo now. I promise to keep the ring safe, on one condition.'

Jessie raised her eyebrows. 'What's that?'

'You meet me at the Trevi Fountain at eleven o'clock tomorrow morning. I have a camera crew booked.'

Sophia's eyes widened. 'A camera crew?'

'That's right. We're taking shots of my latest jewellery collection. It would be remiss of me not to escort you around Rome while you're here. I will buy you lunch after the shoot and show you the sights.'

15

TIME TO RELAX

It was after ten o'clock when Jessie and Sophia stepped inside a trattoria. The place was busy and alive with music. Jessie read the menu. 'I've never seen so many types of pizza; I'm so hungry I could eat two!'

Sophia giggled. 'Let's order different ones; then we can share. We can have gelatos for dessert. Ice cream in Italy is out of this world!'

Jessie let out a sigh. 'I'm pleased the ring's in safe hands now. I'm also delighted you're not engaged to Gino Constantini! Piers was crestfallen when he heard your plans.'

'Piers?'

Jessie gulped her wine. 'You must know that Piers has a soft spot for you.'

Sophia lowered her eyes. 'Well, we had a "moment" when I gave him a tour of the manor.'

Jessie leaned forward. 'Do tell!'

'We would have kissed if mamma hadn't barged into the room.'

Jessie did a little clap. 'You could do a lot worse than Piers, you know.' Jessie considered divulging Piers' plans to Sophia but held herself back from gossiping. By the time she'd finished her glass of wine, she was ready to tell all, 'Piers has not only fallen in love with you at first sight but also wants to buy Hinchingthorpe Manor to use as a family home.'

Sophia poured Jessie another glass of wine. 'Go on. Tell me more.'

'He's even asked your mother for your hand in marriage and promised her a Granny Annex. Emilio's delighted – he'd love Piers as a brother-in-law.'

Sophia's heart was pounding. 'I overheard mamma saying something about that to Emilio. Can Piers afford to buy the manor?'

Jessie nodded. 'He's a multi-millionaire.'

Sophia burst into tears. 'I've been so stupid flying over here to be with a man I don't love. Piers will be disappointed in me.'

Jessie held Sophia's hand. 'Piers admires your fire and passion. He's been around the world and hasn't found anyone like you. He's mature enough to wait for you to go home to the Cotswolds, marry him, and bring lots of little cricket players into the world. He's keen on the game. It's perfect that the manor has a pitch and a pavilion – even though there are rumours of a ghost.'

Sophia giggled. 'You're good for me, Jessie. I'll fly back in the morning and won't tell a soul about what you've just told me. I'll let things take their natural course.'

Jessie slumped back in her chair. 'What about the Trevi Fountain?'

Sophia was messaging on her phone. 'I'm swapping places with Emilio. If he gets the early morning flight, he can be here in time to escort you to the Trevi Fountain. I'm asking him to book my flight home too – on expenses, of course.'

*

Back at Hinchingthorpe Manor, Emilio and Piers were consoling Maria. 'I've worn that ring for years, and now I miss it. I've warded off the attention of numerous gentlemen by pretending to be engaged. Men – I ask you. I've had no time for them bringing up three children on my own. Sophia was the worst – always so strong-willed.'

Piers reached over and patted Maria's hand. 'Tell me more about Sophia.'

'Well, it would take a strong man to tame her. She has a mind of her own and won't be told what's best for her. She should be married by now – she's thirty-four.'

Piers stared at Emilio. 'So Sophia's your older sister.'

Emilio smiled. 'She certainly is. I'm the baby of the family. Luca's thirty-seven.'

Piers took a moment to think. 'What made you leave the nest? It sounds like the manor has been home to your family for years.'

Emilio opened his mouth, and Maria spoke for him. 'Emilio may be the baby of the family, but he's the one who realised we wouldn't all survive if we stayed in a place like this. He set out to make a fortune to provide for us in our old age.'

Emilio coughed. 'That isn't quite true, Mamma. Sophia and Luca can cope on their own. I was just keen to make sure you're OK. I was planning on buying you a nice little cottage when you retired.'

Maria scoffed before walking out of the room. 'But I'm never leaving here. The manor's my home!'

Emilio turned to face Piers. 'See what I'm up against? Sophia has inherited her stubbornness from our mother.'

Piers chuckled. 'No wonder you ran off to the bright lights of London.'

Emilio sighed. 'Are you having second thoughts about buying this place? I'll understand if that's the case. My family are *my* problem.'

Piers shook his head. 'There's no doubt in my mind I want to retire here and bring up a family.'

'But what if Sophia rejects your advances?'

'She won't. We have a connection.'

Emilio's phone beeped with a message. He read it before smiling at Piers. 'Sophia's coming home in the morning. She's asked me to swap places with her.'

'You're going to Rome?'

'To the Trevi Fountain, to be precise. Giuseppe has a photoshoot for his latest jewellery collection tomorrow. He's invited Jessie to join him, and then he's planning on showing her the sights. Sophia thinks he has eyes for her.'

'For Sophia?!'

'No. For Jessie. What am I going to do? I've tried

to put a wedge between any eligible bachelor and Jessie, and the wedges keep disappearing.'

Piers frowned; Emilio wasn't handling this well. Jealousy was clouding his judgement. 'As I've said before, you must give Jessie room to fly. She's young and has great potential in the real estate world. You should be encouraging her to grow – not suppressing her.'

Emilio concentrated on booking his flight for tomorrow. He knew Piers was right, but he didn't like being told how to behave, especially by a team member. Piers could be so high and mighty at times. The sooner he retired, the better.

16

TREVI TEMPTATION

Emilio jumped out of a taxi and rushed through the hotel foyer. He checked in, left his overnight bag in his room, and sprinted down the corridor to knock for Jessie. 'It's me! I just made it in time. The taxi's waiting outside to take us to the Trevi Fountain.'

Jessie opened her door wearing Antoine Chambray's little black dress. Emilio was stunned. 'Why are you wearing that? It's November – you'll be freezing outside.'

Jessie grabbed her coat. 'Giuseppe's been on the phone this morning and convinced me to wear it. He'd seen it on Claudette and thought it would show off some of his jewellery designs.'

'How did Giuseppe know you have it?'

'He was talking to Antoine last night, and he

advised him. They both know I haven't been home since Paris, so it's obvious I'd have it with me.'

'You could have left it at the manor.'

'Why would I leave it there? When I leave Rome, I'm going straight back to the office. We have a job to do, remember? My feet haven't touched the ground since Wednesday. I'm sure I didn't sign up for all of this.'

'What about your car? That's still in the Cotswolds.'

Jessie shrugged. 'Minor issue. We can get it back somehow.' Jessie glared at Emilio. 'I thought you'd be pleased I'm keeping a high-profile client happy *and* that I'm keen to return to normality and catch up with my day job. Your idea that we took time out from work has created this mess.'

'What mess?'

'Too much work and too little time to keep on top of things. Come on, or we'll be late.'

Emilio let Jessie fly past him. He made sure her bedroom door was locked, then rushed after her. Jessie was stressed. She'd been working non-stop. At least *he'd* had a day off yesterday and felt relatively refreshed. It was best to keep his head down while Jessie was like this; he wasn't used to her being so assertive.

As soon as the pair climbed out of the taxi, Giuseppe strode over to greet them. He shook hands with Emilio, then placed an arm around Jessie. 'We need to get you into hair and makeup. Things aren't going quite to plan this morning; Fantasia fell down the Spanish Steps.'

Jessie gasped. 'Goodness, who's Fantasia? Is she OK?'

'Fanta's a supermodel; you must have heard of her. She was nearly at the bottom of the steps when she fell and only twisted her ankle. We were taking some shots there before we set up at the fountain.'

Jessie was about to deny any knowledge of Fantasia when a tall willowy brunette appeared from behind Emilio and slid her arm through his. 'Emilio! Long time no see. I'm so pleased you're here. I need a walking stick, or a crutch, or a wheelchair. Unfortunately, Giuseppe hasn't found me anything suitable yet. That means *you'll* have to do. Let's go for a coffee. I need to get my ankle out of the cold. I won't mind if you carry me.'

Jessie was shocked to see a smiling Emilio throw his arm under Fanta's legs and lift her into the air. 'Coffee sounds like a great idea. It's far too cold to be outside today in a backless dress.'

Fanta giggled. 'I'm not wearing a backless dress.

You cheeky thing.'

Emilio felt Jessie's glare boring into the back of his head as he carried the injured supermodel into the warmth of a cosy coffee shop.

Giuseppe guided Jessie through an arched doorway which led into a vast marble-tiled entrance hall with wrought iron staircases and an abundance of greenery. Jessie caught her breath at the opulence. There were dressing tables, screens, clothes racks, models, makeup artists, and hairdressers.

Jessie felt nervous. 'I'm not going to have to wear different clothes, am I? I'm not a supermodel shape.'

Giuseppe put her at ease as he handed her a white faux fur jacket. 'I'll only need you to wear this, so you don't get cold. You can take it off for some shots and drape it over an arm or shoulder. Antoine's dress and my jewellery are a match made in heaven. There's no need to overcomplicate things.'

*

From a window seat in the coffee shop, Emilio admired the scenery. Stunning models were draped around the Trevi fountain with frozen smiles, while onlookers and photographers were blue with the cold. Emilio smiled to himself; Jessie would regret wearing that dress. He rubbed his cold hands together, then sank back in his chair to enjoy a hot cappuccino and almond biscotti.

It was great to see Fanta again. She had an uncanny knack of massaging Emilio's ego – which he appreciated after such a taxing week. Emilio was still recovering from Claudette's loss, never mind Jessie's aloofness this morning. He'd flown to Rome to be with Jessie. She could at least have shown some appreciation rather than try to pick a fight.

Gasps and screams from the crowd of onlookers alerted the waiting paparazzi to the arched doors of the changing area opening and the famous jewellery designer walking through with Jessie on his arm. Cameras flashed as Giuseppe bent down to kiss Jessie on her cheek. More camera flashing and excitement followed when Giuseppe helped Jessie off with her fur jacket and adjusted her necklace. The smile didn't leave Giuseppe's annoyingly smug face. Emilio was agitated.

Fanta's brunette hair fell to her waist, and she twisted a clump around her finger while trying to attract Emilio's attention. 'Stop looking out of the window and give me an answer.'

Emilio turned to face her. 'What?'

'Will you come with me to Mexico for my next shoot? I'll need a companion in case my ankle gives way.'

Emilio shook his head. 'Too much work, I'm

afraid.'

Fanta tutted. 'When did you become so boring? You used to be such fun. All work and no play is making you a very dull boy. You're getting lines around your eyes – you used to be so handsome.'

Emilio rubbed his face. 'Am I? Lines? Well, I *have* been working around the clock.' Emilio glanced at Giuseppe, who was all over Jessie, and he felt like a spare part. 'Well, I was planning to stay in Rome and deal with a client, but one of my agents can handle it. You're right. I need some time out.'

Fanta shrieked with delight. 'Goodie! I'll get my manager to make the arrangements.'

'When will we need to leave?'

'This afternoon.'

'How long will we be away?'

Fanta reached over to squeeze Emilio's hand before winking at him. 'As long as it takes for you to fall in love with me again.'

Emilio smiled. He'd missed this – women falling at his feet. Jessie didn't have the time or the inclination to give him what he needed. Piers was right. Jessie should be set free to find her niche. She'd either fly high or fall low.

Emilio sent a message to his team:

> *I have urgent business to attend to this week. I'm leaving Piers in charge until I get back. Keep up the good work! Emilio*

17

BACK IN THE OFFICE

On Wednesday morning, Jessie walked into the London office of *Rawlinson's Residential* to a round of applause. That was a far cry from a week ago when Guy and Nate had mocked her for not bringing in enough listings. There was a massive bouquet on her desk from Giuseppe for helping him with the photoshoot and a framed black and white photograph on the wall of the pair of them next to the Trevi Fountain.

Nate smiled. 'We printed that photograph off as soon as we saw it. Giuseppe's put it on the front page of his website, *and* it's been in the press. Publicity like that is huge. We're already getting enquiries on the back of your romantic rendezvous in Rome!'

Jessie laughed. 'Stop exaggerating. No one knew who I was, or which business I worked for.'

Guy held out his phone to show Jessie a press article which read:

> *Giuseppe Firenzo highly recommends Rawlinson's Residential (London) to manage your property portfolios. Giuseppe said: 'Rawlinson's go above and beyond meeting their client's needs. My agent, Jessie, did not hesitate to help with my recent photoshoot in Rome. I'm sure you will agree that Jessie looks amazing in an Antoine Chambray dress.'*

Jessie gulped. 'That was so kind of Giuseppe. I'll need to thank him.'

The sight of Piers sitting at Emilio's desk made Jessie's heart sink. She couldn't believe Emilio had just upped and left Rome to run off with a supermodel. He didn't even say "goodbye". All the excitement of Sunday morning dispersed as soon as she read Emilio's message to the team. She'd had to compose herself before advising Giuseppe that it would just be her viewing his palazzo and discussing his property portfolio before flying back to London on Tuesday evening. She had to admit that things had gone far better than expected. She'd been thrown in at the deep end but survived. It was a bonus that Giuseppe made time to have the ring assessed, and she had an envelope in her bag to give to Maria with the valuation.

It was lunchtime before Piers got a chance to speak to Jessie. He was keen to discover why there had been a sudden change to Emilio's plans. He grabbed his coat and walked over to her desk. 'Fancy a bite to eat? I'll pay as I'm effectively your boss this week.'

Jessie stood up. 'That would be great. I have an envelope to give Maria and need to get my car back from Hinchingthorpe Manor. Are you planning to go back there soon?'

Piers smiled. 'I'm sure I can help you. We can discuss over lunch.'

Piers held the office door open for Jessie to walk through first. Then, as soon as they were outside, he turned to face her. 'What made Emilio leave Rome and abandon the business like that? He didn't mention anything to me. I just got the same message as everyone else. I'd have stayed in the Cotswolds if I didn't have to return to London to cover for him.'

Jessie felt the same irritation as Piers. 'He didn't tell me anything either. One minute he was in a coffee shop near the Trevi Fountain with a supermodel called Fanta. The next, he was gone. He didn't stay around to meet with Giuseppe. He left it all to me. I'm so annoyed with him.'

Piers opened the door to a café. 'Step inside. I might be able to piece things together.'

After the couple had placed their orders, Piers spoke quietly and waited for Jessie's reaction, 'Emilio and Fanta were engaged.'

Jessie's eyes widened. 'What?!'

'They were engaged for six months before Emilio met Claudette and broke things off with Fanta.'

Jessie was shocked. Emilio was nothing like she'd assumed. She'd thought there was chemistry between them, but now it was apparent Emilio had a whole chemistry set at his disposal that worked with any woman he set eyes on. How could she have been so gullible?

Piers could see her anger. 'If it's any help, Emilio likes you. You're different to the type he normally goes for. Emilio was jealous about you spending time with Giuseppe. He even tried to keep you away from Antoine and Logan. I told him to set you free so that you could spread your wings. The worst thing he could do was suppress you. You need to stretch yourself to see how far you can go.'

Jessie wasn't pacified. 'Well, as far as I'm concerned, Emilio is rude, obnoxious, and reckless. He's not my type. I prefer stability in a man, someone who's strong and mature and knows what he wants. Not someone who goes off in a strop and plays games.'

Piers couldn't argue with Jessie's summary of

Emilio's behaviour, so he changed the subject. 'I'm going back to the Cotswolds on Friday night. I'll be spending the weekend with Sophia. If you give me your car keys, I'll go there on the train and drive your car back on Sunday.'

Jessie let out a sigh of relief. 'That's great, thanks, Piers.' Jessie reached inside her bag and took out her car keys and the envelope from Giuseppe. 'Please give this to Maria while you're there, then she can decide what she wants to do about the ring.'

Piers tucked the envelope into his jacket pocket. 'Of course. Is there anything else I can do for you?'

Jessie felt a weight lifting from her shoulders now that Emilio was temporarily out of the picture. 'Yes, Piers, there is. I need you to pass on your knowledge and expertise before you retire. Please teach me how to fly.'

Piers felt flattered by Jessie's request. 'It will be my pleasure. You can be my protégé. The real estate world won't know what's hit it.'

Jessie giggled. 'I'm excited already!'

*

After a week of playing "catch up", following the team's event in the Cotswolds, the weekend couldn't come quick enough for the agents at *Rawlinson's*

Residential. It was, therefore, an unwelcome intrusion when Emilio booked a last-minute video call with the London office at four o'clock on Friday.

Everyone sat around a large screen in the boardroom and waited until Emilio's tanned face popped up. As if to rub salt into the wound, Emilio was sitting on a beach with a jug of fresh orange juice and a bowl of fruit in the background, not to mention a raft of palm trees shading him from the sun.

Jessie narrowed her eyes when he waved from the screen and said, 'Buenos días, everyone!'

The rest of the team wavered between scowling and muttering obscenities. Emilio picked up a banana, peeled it, and bit the end off. Speaking with his mouth full, he dared to ask, 'What's wrong? I thought you'd be pleased I took time out to check in with the team. How are the results for this week? Where's Piers?'

Jessie took the lead. 'The results for this week have never been better. Clients are queuing up to work with us to the extent that we need to recruit additional staff. The business pipeline is healthy beyond measure, and we all need to finish for the weekend soon to recharge our batteries. Concerning Piers, he's been a star this week. His maturity and expertise have held our business together.'

Emilio choked on his banana before speaking,

'Where *is* Piers? I can't see him on the screen.'

Jessie nudged Nate, who nudged Guy, who pulled the plug out of the internet connection. The move was swift and seamless. Jessie stood up before speaking to her colleagues. 'Oh dear, I didn't get chance to advise Emilio that Piers left slightly early to catch a train. We should all ensure we get away from here by five o'clock tonight. Well done, everyone, it's been a great week!'

18

HELP REQUIRED

On Saturday, Jessie woke at eight o'clock. She stretched her arms and legs and relished the thought that she had nothing to do today. It was busier than usual in London at this time of the year. With just over a month until Christmas, the main shopping areas would be packed. Jessie only needed to buy some Christmas cards and a pint of milk, so popping to the corner shop before breakfast seemed the best thing to do. She could buy fresh croissants as a treat.

After pulling on her hat, scarf, and gloves, she wrapped her coat around her and left her house with her purse, phone, and keys. What she hadn't accounted for was that she may bump into someone when she was wearing no makeup. After smiling at the shopkeeper and picking up a carton of milk, Jessie felt a tug on the hemline of her coat. She turned around to see two small children staring up at her with wide eyes. 'We've lost our uncle.'

Jessie bent down to face the children. 'When did you last see your uncle? What are your names?'

A man bent down next to Jessie. 'They saw me thirty seconds ago in the fruit and veg aisle. Their names are Matty and Mason. They're four and five years old and have been giving me the run around since six o'clock yesterday evening.'

Jessie giggled and turned to face the man before being shocked to the core. 'Logan! What are you doing here?'

Logan was shocked too. 'Jessie! I didn't recognise you.'

Jessie blushed. 'I look different without makeup.'

Logan spluttered. 'No, it's not that. I think it's the hat.'

Jessie stood up. 'Well, I'd best be on my way. I only came out for a pint of milk. Have a good day!'

Mason pulled on his uncle's sleeve. 'Can Jessie come shopping with us?'

Logan's mouth fell open, and Jessie tried to

alleviate the awkwardness. 'That's very kind of you, but I'm busy this morning. I must dash.' Jessie paid for the milk and waved to Logan and his nephews as she exited the shop.

Closing her front door behind her, Jessie was shocked to see the state of herself in her hall mirror. It wasn't surprising Logan hadn't initially recognised her. She'd go out later to buy Christmas cards and make do with toast instead of croissants for breakfast. That was a small price to pay to limit the embarrassment she'd felt when she'd bumped into one of *Rawlinson's Residential*'s premier clients. A thought entered Jessie's mind. Wasn't Logan supposed to be running off to Gretna Green with Fiona this weekend? She rubbed her forehead; it had been such a mind-blowing week that she couldn't remember exactly when he was supposed to be getting married. Her heart sank at the thought. She frowned as she turned on the radio. Why would she feel upset about that?

Biting into her toast, she couldn't get the thought of bumping into Logan, not once but twice, out of her mind. Both times had been embarrassing; there was Wednesday night in Paris when he'd helped her with the necklace, and she'd accidentally rubbed her hair against his face; then there was this morning when he'd seen her looking her worst. Jessie allowed herself a small smile when she thought of how charming he'd been on both occasions.

Jessie finished her breakfast and decided to chill out on the sofa. She placed a cushion under her head and tried to relax after a rollercoaster of a week. When she closed her eyes, a vision came into her head: Logan and Fiona running through fields of heather in Scotland. Logan wearing a kilt, and Fiona a wedding dress. Logan bending down to kiss his bride, his sandy hair shining in the sun and his sparkling green eyes enhanced by attractive laughter lines. Jessie could almost smell the heather – no, it wasn't the heather. She sniffed her hand – it was Logan's aftershave. Jessie sat up with a start and sniffed her hand again. She'd taken her glove off to shake hands with him before she went to pay for the milk. Logan must have splashed aftershave on before going to the shop.

Jessie was annoyed with herself for feeling so deflated. She needed to spring into action. This wasn't like her at all. She was tired from a taxing week. First job was to load the dishwasher. Then she would shower and do her hair and makeup before going to the shop again to buy cards. After that, she would spend the afternoon watching a Christmas film. Tonight she would write the cards while drinking wine and eating pizza. There! A full day ahead and no time to dwell on thoughts of Logan Charteris.

Two hours later, Jessie was pulling on her coat to leave the house again when her phone rang. It was Logan – her heart leapt! 'Hi, Logan. I didn't expect to hear from you again today. I know how busy you are with your nephews.'

Logan sounded stressed. 'I really don't like to ask, but Mason and Matty are insisting they give you your glove back in person. I told them I would drop it into your office or give it to Guy when I next see him. I've been putting up with their tantrums for over two hours now, and they won't take "no" for an answer.'

Jessie giggled. She glanced in the hall mirror; she looked a different person from the one who went out this morning. 'Well, I'm not sure your nephews will recognise me now. I've taken off my hat, and I'm wearing makeup.'

Logan's voice sounded calmer. 'You look great with or without makeup.'

Jessie laughed. 'Where should I meet you?'

'We're in Hamleys. We're due to see Santa in his festive grotto at noon. I don't suppose you could make it in time for that?'

Jessie closed the door behind her and hailed a taxi. 'I'm on my way!'

Jessie walked through the toy shop twenty minutes later with a spring in her step. Santa's Festive Grotto was well signposted, and the boys spotted her before she saw them. They ran up to her and hugged her legs.

'Jessie! You came!'

Matty held out Jessie's glove with a big grin on his face. 'You dropped this, and I found it.'

Jessie took hold of her glove and smiled back at him. 'Thank you so much. My hand has been ever so cold. You boys are little angels.'

Logan raised his eyebrows at that comment. Mason didn't agree with Jessie either, 'No, we're not. We're Superheroes.' He punched the air and did a twirl to prove his point.

Logan checked the time. 'We should get in the queue to see Santa. We can't keep him waiting.'

With the boys chatting to each other excitedly, Logan turned to Jessie. 'I'm sorry about this. I know you said you were busy this morning. I'm relieved you managed to make it, or I'd have been dragging them kicking and screaming into Santa's Grotto. I'd been doing well until you lost your glove. I only have two hours left until I return the boys to my sister and brother-in-law.'

Jessie stared into Logan's sparkling eyes, and her stomach lurched when she realised he was looking deep into her soul. 'How's Emilio doing?'

Jessie dropped her eyes. 'He's on the other side of the world with a supermodel.'

The queue started moving forward. Logan was shocked. 'What?'

'Her name's Fantasia. Fanta for short.'

'Are you upset about that?'

'Why would I be upset?'

'I thought there may be something going on between you two.'

Jessie huffed. 'Emilio's not my type.'

Logan stared into her eyes again. 'What *is* your type?'

'Someone who knows what he wants. A strong man with high morals. A man who wants me.'

Mason and Matty had stepped forward in the queue – prompting an elf to interrupt Jessie and Logan's conversation. 'Your children are on their way to see Santa. If you're quick, we can take a family photo.'

Logan grabbed Jessie's hand and dragged her through a tunnel lit with fairy lights. The boys were standing in front of Santa, and Logan manoeuvred a reluctant Jessie to stand with him behind Santa's chair. He placed his arm around her, and a photographer captured a shot.

Jessie's mind was spinning. What would Fiona say?! If it were Jessie getting married to Logan any day now, she wouldn't want him visiting Santa with some random woman. Jessie was surprised Logan was being so reckless. She felt a small hand slide into hers and looked down to see Matty smiling up at her. Mason was holding onto Logan. They made their way out of the festive grotto, through the shop and onto the pavement. Jessie was at a loss for words until she overheard Mason talking to Logan, 'You're my favourite uncle, so I asked for a present for you.'

Logan smiled. 'That's very kind of you, Mason. What did you ask for?'

'A girlfriend.'

Matty pulled on Jessie's arm. 'I asked Santa for *you* to be Uncle Logan's girlfriend.'

Jessie and Logan stood with flushed faces as the boys argued. Mason was adamant that the idea of a girlfriend had been his, and Matty said *his* idea was better as he'd ensured Santa would bring the right one.

Logan sighed. 'I have another ninety minutes of this. Would you like to join us for lunch? I've promised to buy the boys pizza.'

Jessie shook her head. 'I'll make a quick getaway if you don't mind – I'm having pizza for dinner.' She bent down to smile at Mason and Matty. 'I hope you have a nice lunch with your uncle. Thank you for finding my glove; I'll have warm hands now all the way home.' Jessie waved and then headed for the tube station.

It was four o'clock when Jessie received another call from Logan. 'It's me again. Fiona would like to meet you. Is there any chance you could join us near the London Eye at six o'clock?'

Jessie gulped. She wasn't surprised Fiona wanted to meet her – how embarrassing. Jessie felt very annoyed with Logan for getting them into such a difficult situation. If Logan weren't a client of *Rawlinson's Residential*, she'd tell him where to go.

Logan could hear Jessie sigh down the phone before trying to sound happy about the situation. 'How lovely. I'll see you at six.'

19

NEW BEGINNINGS

Jessie changed into the pale blue dress Sophia had bought for her in Rome. She would wear it under her cream cashmere coat and pretend she was going out tonight. That way, she could make a quick getaway. Jessie had said she was having pizza for dinner – *they* didn't know it was frozen and that she would eat alone. She'd let Logan and Fiona think she was off out on a hot date to an Italian restaurant.

Jessie looked in her hall mirror again before closing her front door. This was the last thing she wanted to be doing on a Saturday night. Fiona would let rip at her for spending time with her fiancé, particularly if Mason and Matty had divulged their Christmas wishes. Jessie was sure Logan had said he was running away with Fiona this weekend; they must be heading off to Gretna Green soon.

As Jessie approached the London Eye, she saw Logan's shiny sandy hair standing out from the crowd. He stood with his arm around Fiona, and they were laughing. They looked happy in each other's company, and Jessie didn't feel so bad about being introduced. Maybe she hadn't caused a rift between them.

Logan waved to her. 'Jessie! Come and meet Fiona.'

Jessie smiled as she walked up to shake Fiona's hand, but Fiona went in for an embrace. 'Jessie! It's so good to meet you. The boys didn't do you justice when they described you. They said you wore a hat and gloves. You have beautiful blonde hair and such pretty blue eyes.'

Fiona let go of Jessie and went to hug Logan. 'Thanks for arranging for me to meet Jessie. I must jump in the taxi now, or we'll miss our flight.' Fiona kissed Logan on his cheek and smiled at Jessie. 'I hope to see you again soon.'

Logan's eyes followed Fiona as she climbed into a taxi containing a man and two boys. He waved as it drew away, then turned to face Jessie. 'Come with me, or we'll miss *our* flight.'

Jessie's mouth fell open as Logan escorted her into a private pod on the London Eye. Her eyes lit up at the sight of champagne and canapes. Her heart was pounding, and her head was racing. She couldn't possibly make sense of what was happening.

Logan handed her a glass of champagne. 'Fiona is my sister. I'm not running off to Gretna Green with anyone. I'm very close to my family, and when I get married, it will be a big wedding – unless my bride chooses otherwise.'

Noticing the colour had drained from Jessie's face, Logan took the glass from her and slid an arm around her waist. 'Would you like to sit down?'

Jessie shook her head. 'I'm all right with you holding me up.' When Logan's news had sunk in, the colour began to return to Jessie's cheeks. 'Why did you make up such a story about getting married?'

Logan ran a hand through Jessie's hair as he spoke. His eyes didn't leave hers for a moment. 'Because Emilio's got it bad for you. He effectively put up walls between you, Antoine, Giuseppe, and me in a matter of hours. I decided to remove myself from the scenario before I got hurt.'

Jessie leaned her head against Logan's chest; she couldn't believe this was happening. She could hear his heart beating as she breathed in the familiar smell of his aftershave. Jessie felt him stroke her hair. 'Are you OK?' Jessie nodded, and Logan continued, 'When you mentioned today that Emilio was on the other side of the world with a supermodel, I couldn't believe my luck. I'd stepped away to give my friend a chance with you, and he blew it. I don't intend stepping away again.'

Jessie was becoming acclimatised to her surroundings; they were now at the top of the London Eye, and she didn't want to miss the whole experience by being in a daze. She lifted her head and smiled up at Logan. 'I can't believe we're on the London Eye in a private pod! You can let go of me now. My knees aren't weak anymore. It was just the shock of it all. We should admire the view.'

There was only one view Logan wanted to admire, and she was standing next to him. He watched Jessie tuck into a canapé and suddenly remembered she was having pizza for dinner. His heart sank. Was she about to jump out of the pod when it reached ground level and go off on a hot date? Had he made a complete fool of himself? Jessie turned to look at him and noticed the frown on his face. 'What's wrong?'

Logan lowered his eyes. 'I've been very presumptuous. I've made it clear how I feel about you, but I have no idea if you're interested in me.'

Jessie reached up to brush Logan's fringe away from his sparkling green eyes. 'I'm very interested.'

Logan didn't need further confirmation as he

brushed his lips against Jessie's. 'That's all we have time for before the pod lands. I'll make up for it later.'

*

Over dinner in an intimate Covent Garden restaurant, Jessie and Logan took time to learn about one another. Jessie explained that she'd only been working in real estate for six months and, before she went on the "course" in the Cotswolds, she was the lowest performer in the team. Events had taken a surprising turn, though, and now she could see herself performing alongside the best agents in the business. Piers was doing wonders for her confidence, and she wanted to learn as much as possible from him before he retired.

Logan was impressed by Piers' wisdom and maturity and less so by the irresponsible actions of Emilio. How could a boss use his team to benefit his family by sending them on a fictitious course? He'd also suppressed an employee and then ran off with a supermodel leaving his business to run itself. Logan shook his head in disbelief.

Jessie stared at him. 'I feel bad telling you about Emilio, but now you're more than just a client, you need to know what's happening.'

Logan reached over the table and took hold of Jessie's hand. 'You've done the right thing. I'm just shocked Emilio's acting so recklessly. He's a bit young for a mid-life crisis.'

Jessie tried to lighten the mood. 'Well, Emilio's certainly having fun with whatever he's up to; he messaged the team this afternoon to say he'll be out of the country for another week. That gives me more time with Piers to polish up my real estate skills.'

Logan smiled. 'I like Piers. It's very good of him to bring your car back from the Cotswolds tomorrow. Do you think he has a chance with Sophia?'

Jessie grinned. 'He has an excellent chance with Sophia. They're a perfect match.' Logan squeezed Jessie's hand. He hoped she thought that they were a perfect match too.

Logan had some news for Jessie, 'I heard from Guy this afternoon. He's sold my property in Scotland.'

Jessie squeezed Logan's hand back. 'That's wonderful news! Do you have another property in mind to buy?'

Logan's eyes twinkled. 'Nate's found one for me. Antoine's selling his London townhouse, and there's an open house for potential buyers on Tuesday evening. I've said I'll pop along. I've been briefed to wear black tie. It must be quite an event.'

Jessie's eyes widened. 'I'll be there. All our agents

are going. Nate's pulling out all the stops to make a quick sale for Antoine. There'll be a pianist, opera singer, and buffet prepared by a Michelin Star chef – to name but a few of the surprises in store.'

Logan held Jessie's gaze. 'They're not surprises anymore.'

Jessie blushed. 'I'm sorry.'

Logan smiled as he rubbed her fingers. 'Will you be wearing Antoine's dress?'

Jessie kept a straight face. 'If I tell you, it won't be a surprise. Anyway, why are you looking to buy a house in London? I thought you were based in Scotland.'

Logan shrugged. 'It makes sense. Since things have taken off with the hotel chain, I spend most of my time in London – apart from when I'm needed in Paris or New York – I should have made the move sooner.'

Jessie was thrilled at the news but tried not to show it. She removed her hand from Logan's and picked up the dessert menu. 'I'm not sure I could eat a whole dessert. Would you like to share one?'

Logan scanned his copy of the menu. 'As long as it's the sticky toffee pudding, and I get the largest portion.'

Jessie giggled. 'Sounds perfect to me.'

20

OPEN HOUSE

On Tuesday evening, Antoine's London townhouse was a hive of activity. Antoine had left the event for potential buyers in the capable hands of the agents at *Rawlinson's Residential* while he concentrated on his latest fashion collection. He rarely used the house in London these days, so it made sense to sell it and make better use of his capital elsewhere.

Nate was buoyant as he greeted potential buyers; his commission payment for the sale of this house would exceed the amount Guy made last week for selling Logan's property in Scotland. Jessie's brief trip to Paris had benefitted the whole team! Nate would be throwing a thirtieth birthday bash like no other at this rate.

Guy stood next to Jessie. 'Aren't you going to take your coat off?'

Jessie's eyes darted around the room. 'I regret wearing this dress.'

Guy frowned. 'What's wrong with it?'

Jessie sighed. 'It's one of Antoine's designs, so I felt it was appropriate to wear it tonight. The only trouble is, it's such a stunning dress that I feel I'm the centre of attention when I'm wearing it.'

Piers walked over with two glasses of champagne. He handed one to Jessie. 'What's wrong?'

Guy grinned. 'Jessie's wearing one of Antoine's creations, and now she's worried she'll steal the limelight at Nate's event.'

With Guy's attention diverted to a client, Piers offered Jessie advice, 'Lesson one in flying is: Believe in yourself, have confidence in your abilities, and hold your head high so everyone else believes in you too. It's all about having an aura – you're a shining light. Never allow yourself to think otherwise.'

Jessie fiddled with her silver earrings. She didn't have a necklace that matched them, so she'd decided not to wear one. She turned to look up at Piers. He was a brilliant confidence coach. 'Thanks, Piers. Sophia's very lucky to have you.'

Piers smiled. 'I know.'

Jessie took a deep breath and let her cream cashmere coat fall from her shoulders. She could feel the admiring glances from around the room. Nate walked up to her and let out a low whistle. 'You look amazing.'

Jessie felt relieved by Nate's reaction. 'I only wore it because it's an Antoine Chambray creation. It seemed appropriate to wear it tonight when we're trying to sell his house.' Jessie finished her glass of champagne and reached for another one. She glanced around the room, but there was no sign of Logan.

Nate was buoyant as he spoke, 'I can't believe the take-up we've had for tonight's open house. I thought Piers' idea of a black tie event would put some buyers off, but I couldn't have been more wrong.' Piers overheard Nate's comment and allowed himself a knowing grin. He hadn't made it to the top of the real estate world without knowing what impressed the most demanding of clients.

Nate turned to Jessie. 'With such a great show of interest, I'll recommend to Antoine we sell the property by auction. The more the property goes for, the more commission we'll make; it will easily exceed the asking price.'

Jessie frowned. 'I thought you had this house lined

up for Logan?'

'Yes, I did. But at least fifteen other clients are interested too, and we need to get the best deal for Antoine *and* ourselves. I can't wait to see our sales figures at month end. Emilio will drop through the floor when he realises the business has been more successful without him at the helm. He should go away to far-flung places more often.'

Jessie felt a hand on her shoulder, and she spun around. 'Logan! How lovely to see you.'

Nate reached out to shake Logan's hand while scanning the room for Guy, who was in deep conversation with a group of potential clients. All agents were on duty tonight, so Nate had no hesitation in connecting Jessie to Logan. He smiled at the tall, sandy-haired man in a designer dinner jacket. 'If it's OK with you, Jessie will show you around the property. I know Guy's your usual agent, but we need to spread ourselves around at events like these.'

Logan couldn't wipe the smile from his face as he locked eyes with Jessie. He turned to face Nate. 'If that's the case, then so be it.'

Jessie handed Logan a brochure. 'Everything you need to know about the property is in here.'

Logan didn't take his eyes off her. 'I've viewed it

online.'

Jessie's knees felt weak. Why did Logan do this to her? She had to focus on her job. 'Well, there's nothing better than seeing a property with your own eyes, feeling the smoothness of the marble worktops, making sure there are no doorframes too low for you to walk through, smelling the flowers in the garden.'

Logan chuckled. 'I know how smooth marble is, I'm not a giant, and I doubt there are many flowers in the garden in November.'

Jessie suppressed a giggle before whispering to him, 'I'm just trying to do my job. Let's have a look around. There are so many potential buyers that Nate will call Antoine tomorrow and recommend the property goes to auction. If that happens, it will sell for far beyond Antoine's asking price. Properties like this in London are scarce. Let's go through the motions and enjoy the evening. Other properties on our books may be suitable for you.'

Logan raised an eyebrow. Didn't Jessie think he was rich enough to buy this house at auction? She obviously hadn't realised he *owned* the hotel chain. Logan hadn't gone into much detail when they'd had dinner on Saturday.

After viewing the inside of the property, Logan helped Jessie on with her coat before the couple ventured outside. Logan had to admit the garden was stunning with its ornate trees and marble statues. The outdoor lighting showed it at its best. He turned Jessie to face him before holding her hands in his. 'I have a confession to make.'

Jessie's face dropped; she'd known the fairy tale she'd been living for the last two weeks had to end sometime. What bombshell was Logan going to drop? Was he married? Was he paying maintenance for a raft of children in London, Paris, and New York? Was he penniless and just pretending to be rich? Jessie's knees didn't go weak this time. Instead, her heart sank to the floor.

Logan released Jessie's hands and reached inside his pocket for a box. He held it out to her. 'It's not the original box, but I needed to keep them in something while I worked out what to do for the best.'

Jessie's disappointment turned to intrigue, and she opened the box. Her mouth fell open, and Logan enlightened her on his confession. 'When we were in Paris, you gave these back to Antoine. After you'd made a quick exit, Antoine gave them to me. He said he wanted you to have them, along with the dress. He was unaware he would travel to the Cotswolds with Giuseppe at the time, but he knew I was planning to go there the following day. I've been waiting for the right time for you to accept them.'

Jessie shook her head. 'There's no way I can accept diamonds from Antoine. I gave them back to him in Paris. What's different now for you to think I'll change my mind?'

Logan blushed. 'Because the sale of this house to me will only happen if you accept Antoine's gift.'

Jessie laughed. 'There's no guarantee you'll be able to afford the house when it goes to auction. Every expectation is that it'll go through the roof. Some of our clients are billionaires.'

Logan kept his composure. 'Antoine and I have known each other for years. It wasn't coincidental he chose my hotel in Paris for his cocktail party; I always support his events. When Guy and Nate thought this property was a good fit for me, they were spot on. It was, however, a coincidence that Antoine contacted me this afternoon to ask if I'd passed on the diamonds to you. He suggested a deal when he knew I'd have trouble getting you to accept them.'

Jessie's eyes were on stalks. 'What deal?'

'I buy this house at the full asking price, and you accept the diamonds. Antoine isn't budging. He says it's a crime for you not to wear the diamonds with the dress.'

Jessie gripped the box tightly while she channelled

her thoughts. 'But Nate is going to suggest that the house goes to auction. Antoine may get a better deal.'

Logan shook his head. 'That's not what Antoine wants. If you accept the diamonds, the deal is done.'

Jessie's heart was beating through her chest. She didn't know if it was because Logan's confession had amounted to nothing other than excitement or that she was being forced to accept a set of diamonds that were anybody's dream. Her thoughts turned to Piers – what would he suggest she do? She knew straight away what Piers would say.

Jessie handed the box back to Logan and then removed her silver earrings. 'You'll need to help me with the necklace. I struggle with the clasp.'

21

A SURPRISE VISITOR

While Jessie was in the garden with Logan, Emilio strode through the kitchen and headed for Piers.

Piers stared at him. 'Emilio! Why are you back in the UK so soon?'

Emilio's eyes scanned the room for Jessie. 'Because I've been stupid. Fanta's not a patch on Jessie. Where's my leading agent?'

Piers rubbed his chin while waiting for Emilio's reaction to the news. 'Jessie's showing Logan around the property.'

Emilio scowled. 'But Guy's Logan's agent.'

Piers was becoming tired of Emilio's protective stance over Jessie. 'Not tonight. You know how these events work; the agents have to share themselves around.'

Emilio turned on his heel. 'Well, I'll go and find them. Jessie will be pleased to know I'm back.'

The kitchen doors slid open as Logan followed Jessie into the warmth. He helped her off with her coat, and Guy and Nate had their second shock of the night – Jessie was dripping in diamonds! They'd just seen Emilio striding through the building in search of her, and unknown to everyone, she'd been outside accepting gifts from a client! On top of that, Jessie had the nerve to summon Piers, Nate, and Guy into the study.

She closed the door behind them before speaking, 'Antoine's done a deal directly with Logan. It's nothing to worry about, as the sale will still go through our business, and we'll get the full commission payment. We'll just have to let the event run tonight with our other clients thinking the property's still on the market.'

Piers stared at Jessie with admiration. She was coming on leaps and bounds; he was proud of her. Nate couldn't help but ask, 'Where did you get the diamonds?'

Jessie touched an earring. 'Oh, these. I left them in Paris by mistake, and Logan kindly brought them back for me. I must admit that Antoine's dress needs some sparkle to set it off.'

Piers chuckled to himself at Jessie's newfound confidence. Emilio couldn't hold her back anymore – she was flying high. He left it to Guy to break the news of Emilio's sudden return. 'Well, we've had our week of freedom. The big bad boss is back.'

Jessie raised her eyebrows. 'Emilio's here?'

Nate nodded. 'He certainly is, and he's looking for you.'

Jessie sighed. She wasn't keen to see Emilio after he'd left her in the lurch in Rome and run off with his ex-fiancée. That move had been strictly taboo in Jessie's eyes. It was terrible enough leaving her alone without any explanation; it was disgraceful he'd neglected the business too.

Emilio found Logan in the kitchen. 'Logan! Where's Jessie?'

Logan held out his hand to shake his friend's. So Emilio hadn't stayed with the supermodel for an extra week. It wasn't surprising he was back and turning his attention on Jessie again. Emilio was in for a shock – Jessie was no longer available. Emilio didn't need to wait long; Jessie walked into the kitchen wearing

Antoine Chambray's dress and Claudette's diamonds.

Emilio caught his breath. Jessie had gone back to the cocktail party to return the necklace and earrings. What was going on? Had she been lying to him? He narrowed his eyes as he stared at her. Piers sensed an atmosphere between the two, which wasn't good for business. He took Emilio to one side. 'I was in the Cotswolds at the weekend, and it became evident to me that your mother needs you. Why don't you spend the rest of the week there? I'll travel down again on Friday evening to spend time with Sophia.'

'What's wrong with my mamma?'

'She's coming up with more ghost stories.'

Emilio shrugged. 'So what?'

'She believes them. She was distraught last weekend. Why don't you see her and put her mind at rest? We can do a vigil in the pavilion when I get there at the weekend to prove her thoughts aren't founded.'

'A vigil? Do you mean we should spend all night in the pavilion to prove whether or not my mamma's deluded?'

Jessie had overheard the conversation. 'I think a vigil would be a good idea. I want to put Maria's mind at rest – although I feel she may be onto something. It's spooky in that pavilion. We should hold a vigil on

Saturday and take turns in staying up through the night.'

Logan stepped forward. 'I'm available at the weekend and would be happy to help.'

Guy winked at Nate, who smiled to signify his commitment. 'We'll join you. It sounds like a fun weekend. It's Guy's turn to drive there. I can annoy him with my constant banter while he navigates through fields and hedgerows. That narrow bridge is a shocker, not to mention the cows.'

Emilio couldn't believe he was allowing the team to railroad him. It was unfortunate he needed to stay on the good side of Piers. He needed him to buy the manor. Emilio raised his arms in the air. 'It looks like I have no choice. I'll drive to the manor in the morning and enlist the help of Sophia and Luca for our weekend ghost hunt. It doesn't mean the team can spend the rest of the week slacking. I want Piers to bring the latest sales figures with him on Friday.'

Emilio turned to Jessie. 'We need to speak.' After guiding her to a quiet corner of the kitchen, Emilio blurted out his annoyance, 'You told me you were going back to the cocktail party to return the diamonds to Antoine. Why are they still in your possession?'

Jessie shrugged. 'I *did* return them to Antoine. You can ask Logan. He had to help me take the necklace off as I struggled with the clasp.' Jessie was pleased to see Emilio's eyes ablaze. 'Anyway, Logan helped me again with the necklace tonight as Antoine insists I accept the diamonds as part of the deal for Logan to buy this house. Of course, I couldn't risk losing a deal for the business by refusing to accept a kind offer.'

'How's Logan got involved in all of this?'

'He's friends with Antoine and was hosting the cocktail party at his hotel in Paris.'

'Logan owns that hotel in Paris?'

'He certainly does, and a few others besides. You two need a catch-up. Logan's come far since your university days. It will be good for you to spend time together at the weekend.'

22

RETURN TO THE COTSWOLDS

It had been a difficult few days for Emilio. Not only was he wrestling with his conscience about running off with Fanta, but he was also annoyed that Logan owned a hotel chain and that he'd wormed his way in to deal with Jessie. Emilio couldn't remember when Logan was supposed to run off to Gretna Green. He just hoped it was sooner rather than later. It was unfortunate it wasn't this weekend.

On top of that, Piers had arrived at the manor last night, along with the November sales figures. The business was booming; sales projection going forward was through the roof, and Jessie had the most listings. That made things very difficult for Emilio. Jessie wouldn't look twice at him now she was flying high. He preferred an employee he could nurture, not one who was after his job! He was sure Piers had been encouraging her, but he couldn't fall out with him in case he married into the family. The whole situation was a mess.

Then there was his mamma. She was his biggest worry; Maria was adamant the ghost of the murdered gardener in the cricket pavilion was back. As Piers had said, she seemed pretty upset about the whole thing.

Emilio glanced out of his bedroom window at guests arriving and departing. There was the usual Saturday morning turnaround. He hadn't seen Jessie, Nate, or Guy arrive yet, and he didn't know what car Logan had. Knowing how well his friend was doing, Emilio expected a helicopter to hover overhead before landing on one of the lawns. It wouldn't surprise him if Logan was piloting it himself and had given Jessie a lift. Now that would rub salt into the wound.

Emilio's thoughts were broken by the sound of children. He glanced down to see some poor father leaning into the back of a family car releasing two arguing siblings from their car seats. With the children now kicking at stones in the car park, the man opened the car boot and lifted out a large case which he wheeled with his right arm while holding onto the smallest child with his left. Emilio guessed it was a single father treating his youngsters to a weekend away. He thought bringing them to the manor at the end of November was strange – there would be nothing for them to do – still, each to their own.

Emilio sat at the desk in his room and ploughed through his backlog of emails. He'd had a message earlier from Guy to advise he was on his way with Nate, and they would arrive by eleven o'clock. Emilio was disappointed Jessie hadn't notified him of her estimated arrival time. He guessed she wasn't viewing the weekend as connected to work, and he couldn't blame her for that. How could a ghost hunt be related to real estate?

As if Emilio's mood couldn't drop any further, the worst thing happened. The noisy children were running down his corridor, and their father was unlocking the room next door. There was no soundproofing in this relic of a building, and Emilio decided to get them moved to a different room before they unpacked.

Striding out of his room into the corridor, Emilio knocked on the room next door. He was lost for words when a frazzled Logan opened it. 'Oh, hi Emilio. I had to bring the boys with me at short notice. I promise you'll not even know they're here.'

Emilio's jaw dropped to the floor. His mind was spinning as he composed himself. 'That's OK. I didn't realise you had children. I guess it's your fiancée's hen do this weekend. Being out of the country for a while, I've lost all sense of time and what's happening with our clients. It's very good of you to make the effort to help with the ghost hunt. I'm sure Sophia will look after the children. They will also be a distraction for my mamma.'

Mason shrieked with delight before turning to Matty. 'Ghost hunt! We can be Ghostbusters; wait till we tell everyone at school.'

Matty pushed past Emilio and ran down the corridor. 'Jessie! We're going to be Ghostbusters. Please say you'll help us.'

Emilio frowned; how did Logan's children know Jessie? Jessie bent down to smile at the boys who were clinging to her legs. Mason was keen to show his manners and took hold of Jessie's overnight bag before wheeling it into Logan's room. Jessie giggled. 'Can I have my case back, please? I'm staying in the room opposite.'

Jessie was fully aware of Emilio's angst, and she revelled in it. 'I've just seen Guy and Nate in the car park. Maria says she's given them rooms in this corridor too.' Jessie smiled at the boys, who were looking up at her expectantly. 'Isn't this fun? It's like one big sleepover. I'll drop my bag in my room; then I'll introduce you to everyone. I see you've already met Emilio. We'll bump into Guy and Nate on our way downstairs. Then the only other people to introduce you to are Emilio's mummy, sister, and brother. Oh, and Piers – he works with us.'

Jessie unlocked the door to her room, wheeled her case inside then stepped back into the corridor to hold her hands out for the boys. 'Come along; we'll get a soft drink in the bar. You must be thirsty after such a long journey. We'll give Uncle Logan a rest for half an hour.'

Emilio's eyes darted between Jessie and Logan. He could see a connection between the two. They were very familiar with one another. Logan winked at Jessie as he held a hand to his heart, and Jessie gave Logan a smile that Emilio had never seen before. He watched as Jessie and the children skipped off, then turned to face his old friend. '"Uncle Logan"? I thought the children were yours.'

Logan smiled. 'It feels like they're mine sometimes. My sister tends to take advantage of my childminding services.'

Emilio frowned. 'How does your fiancée feel about that?'

Logan rubbed his chin, he knew the time would come when he'd have to confess, but the way Emilio had behaved recently meant Logan only felt the need to confess to a degree. 'The wedding's off. I'd rather not talk about it.'

The arrival of Guy and Nate was perfectly timed to divert Emilio's attention away from Logan's awkwardness. Guy smiled at Logan. 'We've just met your nephews. Mason and Matty are cool little guys. This could turn into a fun weekend.'

Downstairs, Sophia had taken the boys into the laundry room to find some old sheets. She cut them to suitable sizes and made holes for eyes. Before long, Mason and Matty were running through the foyer, making howling noises. Piers stood next to Jessie. 'Ghosts don't howl, do they?'

Jessie laughed. 'They do if they're called Matty and Mason.'

Emilio walked down the stairs with Logan, Guy, and Nate. The sight of two ghosts running around made his heart sink. How on earth was this vigil thing going to work? It had been Piers' idea that Jessie had fully supported. As far as Emilio was concerned, *they* could sort the whole thing out.

Logan pulled Emilio to one side before handing him a slip of paper. 'Remember Pixie from university?'

Emilio's eyes twinkled. 'Proper Posh Pixie? How could I forget?'

'Well, here's her phone number. She contacted me out of the blue last week to ask if you were available. I said you were, and that this weekend you'd be in the Cotswolds. To summarise, she's cleared her diary to meet you this afternoon for a hot date.' Logan winked at Emilio. 'You should give her a call.'

Emilio held his shoulders back before reaching for his phone. 'I owe you one, Buddy.'

Logan allowed himself a wry smile. He'd contacted numerous university friends to find one that was single and ready to mingle. He'd known he could divert his friend's attention away from Jessie at the drop of a hat – or, rather, the prospect of a new woman. Jessie deserved a better man than Emilio – Jessie deserved to be with Logan.

23

WHO'S THE GHOST?

With Emilio called away on "unexpected business", it was left for Jessie to organise the overnight vigil in the cricket pavilion. It had been Piers' idea, but it was becoming clear he had no clue of how to execute it.

Jessie's starting point was to find out more about the troublesome ghost from Maria. When it was time for Maria's lunch break, Jessie joined her in the kitchen. There was a table for the staff, and Luca had prepared his mother's usual salad lunch. Jessie chatted away while Maria ate her food, and as soon as she'd finished, Jessie turned the conversation to the ghost.

'Please tell me everything you know about the ghost that haunts the cricket pavilion. I understand you're quite upset about it.'

Maria wrung her hands together. 'Promise me you won't tell my children about Bill.'

'Who's Bill?'

'Bill was the gardener. Will you promise me?'

Jessie nodded. 'I promise.'

Maria's eyes scanned the room to ensure no one was in earshot. 'Well, we had a passionate affair. We used to meet in the cricket pavilion at midnight on Tuesdays. The children were tucked up in their beds and never knew.'

Jessie gulped. 'Why Tuesdays?'

'Because Bill only worked on Tuesdays and Saturdays.'

Jessie tried not to laugh. 'Why not Saturdays too?'

'Because I always had an early shift on Sundays.'

Jessie smiled. 'Go on, tell me more.'

'I'm sure he was murdered.'

'Why do you think that?'

'He was found dead in his bed the day after he gave me the ring.'

Jessie raised her eyebrows. 'You said you'd found

the ring in Lost Property.'

'I couldn't tell the truth, could I? When I knew Bill had stolen it from the Lady.'

'The Lady?'

Maria rubbed her forehead. 'It's all a bit of a blur now, but one Saturday night, I heard footsteps on the gravel outside my bedroom window. I peered through the curtains to see the Lady walking towards the cricket pavilion.'

Jessie's mouth fell open. 'What time was that?'

'Just before midnight.'

The women locked eyes, and Maria burst into tears. 'It's been messing with my head for years. I've tried to wipe it from my memory, but Bill was cheating on me.'

Jessie reached over to hold Maria's hand. 'Have you really seen Bill's ghost?'

Maria shook her head. 'I've only imagined it. I was worried he'd come back to haunt me.'

'Why would he want to haunt you?'

'Because, in a mad moment, I told the Lord what he was up to.'

Jessie's head was spinning. No wonder Maria's mind was muddled. She had a question to ask, 'Didn't the Lord and Lady notice you wearing the ring?'

Maria shook her head again. 'They got divorced and sold the manor. It all happened very quickly. There's never been a Lord and Lady since. Once they were gone, I wore the ring every day – Bill was the love of my life. Now that the ring's been taken from me, I'm bereft. I've been having more thoughts that Bill's in the pavilion. He won't be happy I've lost the ring; he took a huge risk taking it from the Lady to give it to me. He won't be resting in peace.'

Jessie's heart went out to Maria. 'We can get the ring back for you. It's yours to do with as you wish. Bill will just be pleased you still love him and have forgiven him for cheating on you.' Jessie rubbed her forehead. 'I'm sure Bill only cheated to get the ring. He loved you very much. There's no need to have thoughts of ghosts anymore. You're free now to enjoy the rest of your life, knowing that Bill would want you to be happy. I understand exactly how you've been feeling, and I will never betray your confidence.'

Maria blew her nose. 'Thank you, Jessie. It's been such a relief to share my thoughts. You've been so understanding.'

Jessie hugged Maria and then searched for the "ghost hunters" who were having lunch in the dining room. She raised her arms in the air. 'The vigil is off. Maria's not seen a ghost; she's just been confused.

Having her ring taken from her has knocked her sideways. She's very attached to it. I'll ask Giuseppe to remove it from his safe and return it to Maria. I'll also suggest to Emilio that he gets it insured.'

Guy sat back in his chair. 'So what are we supposed to do for the rest of the weekend?'

Jessie glanced over at Matty and Mason, tucking into their burgers. 'Well, I've seen a leaflet in Reception advertising a Christmas Fair in the next village. We could go to that this afternoon. And because Emilio's done another runner and left us to our own devices, we should make the most of it. I've spoken to Luca, and he's cooking us Christmas dinner this evening. Champagne will be flowing, and we can pay for the bill on expenses.'

With raised eyebrows around the room, Jessie winked at Piers. 'Emilio hasn't announced yet that Piers is no longer in charge.'

There were cheers all around at that comment.

24

CHRISTMAS FAIR

After wrapping up warm, the group headed to the Christmas Fair. It was a cold afternoon and frosty underfoot. However, the excitement of the festive season brought a warm feeling to everyone. The atmosphere was enhanced by the aroma of mulled wine, roasted chestnuts, and pine trees, which filled the air. Mason and Matty's noses sourced another smell – warm sausage rolls. 'Pleeease, can we have one?!' Logan reached into his pocket for some small change. That should keep the boys quiet for at least twenty minutes.

Guy and Nate headed for the festive coffees hut while Piers and Sophia strolled arm-in-arm around a small market. Jessie wanted to link arms with Logan, but their relationship was still in the early stages, and it was best to keep it under wraps for now. They did their best to share intimate moments in secret – the touch of an arm, a knowing smile, a wink. It was exciting they were the only ones who knew about their budding romance. Jessie spared a thought for Maria and Bill and their hidden affair. Tuesday nights in the cricket pavilion would have been the highlight of Maria's week.

With the boys now riding mechanical reindeer on a carousel and the rest of the group out of sight, Logan stroked Jessie's face as he stared into her eyes. 'Join me in New York for Christmas.'

Jessie's stomach somersaulted, and her heart pounded at Logan's directness and strength of approach. She decided to respond in a similar fashion. 'OK.' Logan's eyes shone as he bent down to kiss her. It couldn't be a long kiss – they were conscious the boys would be circling around on the carousel in less than ten seconds.

By late afternoon the sky had darkened, providing a perfect backdrop for the fairy lights twinkling in the trees, lighting up the market stalls and adorning the fairground rides. Piers' heart pounded as he took Sophia's hand and led her onto a Ferris wheel. He was worried about sharing his news with the amazing woman beside him. What if he'd misjudged Sophia's feelings for him? There was only one way to find out. Piers took a deep breath before looking into Sophia's eyes. 'I've made an offer on the manor, and it's been accepted.'

Jessie had already given Sophia the "heads up" on Piers' intentions when they were together in Rome. She tried to sound surprised. 'Really? Are you thinking of going into the hotel business?'

Piers loosened his scarf, as he continued to gaze into Sophia's eyes. Her reaction to his plan was crucial. 'I'm thinking of getting married and starting a family. I want to turn the manor into a home.'

Sophia let out a nervous giggle. Was Piers trying to gauge her response to that news? Was he trying to propose? Whatever way, he wasn't making it easy for her to comment. She decided to say what she would have said if Jessie hadn't mentioned anything. 'Will I still have a job?'

Piers squeezed her hand. 'Of course, there will always be a place for you, Luca, and Maria at the manor. Don't worry about that.'

Sophia sensed the usually confident Piers was anxious. She liked that; it meant he cared. She tried to lighten the conversation by making a joke. 'Well, when you own the manor, Charles should call you "Lord Hinchingthorpe". He's always called Emilio "Mr Hinchingthorpe".'

Piers raised an eyebrow. 'Why would he do that?'

'Because Charles has known us since we were children. He's always had a soft spot for Emilio.'

Piers blushed. 'I think Charles will have already thought of a name for me. Don't forget I "sacked" him on the first day of the course.'

Sophia giggled. 'That was my fault for making up such a story.'

A fanfare announced the arrival of Santa on his sleigh, causing Mason and Matty to jump up and down while pulling on Logan's coat. 'Can we see Santa, pleeease!'

Logan patted their heads. 'We saw him last week in London, remember? You need to let all the other little children have a go.'

Guy stepped forward. 'Don't be such a spoilsport. Nate and I will take the boys. It's been years since we've seen Santa.'

With Mason and Matty taken care of for the next half hour, Logan bought Jessie a mulled wine. He smiled as he handed it to her. 'I can't wait to get to New York.'

Jessie smiled back. 'Neither can I.'

The queue for Santa wasn't too long, and Mason and Matty decided to be crafty. They would ask this Santa for different presents than the one in London.

That way, they would get more. They just hoped their requirements were relayed correctly to the real Santa in Lapland. The experience took Guy and Nate back to their childhood days. Somehow this weekend in the Cotswolds wasn't turning out too badly after all. They'd been to Hinchingthorpe Manor twice, and on both occasions, the reason for their visit had changed for the better.

Santa took the boys' orders and handed them lollipops before waving them off. Matty licked his lolly and then pulled on Guy's hand. 'We have to go back! We forgot something.'

Mason pulled on Nate's hand too. 'Yikes! We have to go back!'

With the boys pushing to the front of the queue, Guy and Nate could only apologise to the tutting adults. Nate tried to ease the situation. 'We've seen Santa once; this will just be a quick visit. Apologies for any inconvenience.'

Santa frowned at the boys approaching. 'Hello again. What can I do for you?'

Mason took the lead. 'It's not for us this time. We need you to bring Jessie as a present for Uncle Logan.'

Matty nodded in agreement. 'That will make him very happy.'

Santa smiled. 'I'll see what I can do.'

Guy nudged Nate. 'If that happens, it'll be Jessie who's won the lottery. Logan's loaded.'

Nate grinned. 'Jessie's not doing too badly herself. I can't believe the change in her in such a short space of time. It's amazing how being in the right place at the right time can have such an impact. If Emilio hadn't taken her to Paris, Jessie would still be struggling to bring in the listings.'

Guy winked. 'I'm not complaining. We can coast along in her slipstream. I've never had such an easy ride in the real estate business. Long may it continue!'

25

CHRISTMAS PARTY

A table for six had been set in the dining room at Hinchingthorpe Manor. There were Christmas crackers, festive serviettes and table decorations made from holly and ivy cut from the manor grounds. A roaring fire lit up the fireplace, and Christmas music played in the background. With Maria childminding for the evening, Logan could relax.

Sophia encouraged Piers to share his news. 'Tell everyone about your latest purchase.'

Piers swallowed a mouthful of turkey before responding, 'I've had an offer accepted on the manor. I plan to retire here.'

Nate raised his eyebrows. 'We all knew you were

keen on buying the place. You certainly didn't hang around.'

Piers smiled at Sophia. 'I know what I want when I see it. I've been driven by gut feelings my whole life – I've no intention of stopping now.'

Guy raised his glass. 'Well, here's to Piers. The Lord of the Manor.' There were knowing grins from Nate and Jessie at that comment. Piers had risen from the role of gardener to Lord in record time!

Piers had more news. 'I received an interesting message from Emilio before we came down for dinner.'

Nate raised his eyebrows. 'Tell us more.'

'He's discussing with Pixie Pettifer about buying into her business.'

Guy's eyes were alight. 'Pixie Pettifer, the horse trainer?'

Piers nodded. 'Apparently, she wants to buy her brother out of the stud farm they own together, and Emilio's excited about the prospect of moving out of the real estate world into something different.'

Jessie gulped. 'But what will happen to *Rawlinson's Residential*? Will Emilio need to sell it?'

Piers lowered his eyes. 'I believe that's the plan.

Emilio wanted me to make him an offer, but I'm no longer in the position now I'm buying the manor. I'll need extensive funds for the refurbishment of this place.'

Logan cringed. He'd only wanted to get Emilio out of the way for the weekend, not forever. The future of *Rawlinson's Residential* was now in the balance. If the business merged with another agency, jobs could be at risk. What lousy timing Piers had signed on the dotted line for the manor. He would have been the best person to keep the agency afloat.

Maria walked into the dining room with Mason and Matty in their pyjamas. 'These two won't sleep. I've read them several stories. What should I do?'

The boys ran over to Logan before climbing onto his lap. 'Thank you, Maria. You've been a great help. I'll look after them now.'

Mason reached over to grab a holly berry from the table, and Logan stopped him. 'Don't do that. Holly berries are poisonous, and the leaves are very prickly. You could hurt your fingers.'

Matty's eyes widened. 'Did Sleeping Beauty eat a red holly berry?'

Logan shook his head. 'No. She ate a red apple.'

Mason had the next question, 'Did she wake up

when the Prince found her shoe?'

Logan sighed. 'No. That's something to do with Cinderella. Now, come along. We need to get you to bed. Say "goodnight" to everyone.'

Logan held the boys by their hands as he apologised for having to leave the meal. Sophia felt sorry for him. 'I'll arrange for a tray of food to be left outside your room in half an hour. You can't go to bed on an empty stomach.' Logan smiled his appreciation at that and said his goodbyes.

Half an hour later, with the boys fast asleep, Logan opened his bedroom door to collect his food. He was shocked to see a small table with two chairs in the corridor and a smiling Jessie sipping a glass of champagne. She whispered, 'You'll disturb the boys if you eat dinner in the room. I thought I'd keep you company out here. We can have our own Christmas party.'

Two hours later, Guy and Nate returned to their rooms to see Jessie and Logan sitting in the corridor. Logan jumped up. 'You wouldn't mind taking over for a while, would you? Jessie and I could do with some fresh air. We might as well see if there are any ghosts out there tonight, or we'll feel we've missed out on the whole ghost hunting experience.'

Guy raised an eyebrow. 'What's in it for us?'

'I'll get room service to bring you some Scotch whisky.'

Nate nodded his approval. 'Peanuts too?'

'They can be arranged.'

Logan let Jessie walk in front of him down the corridor, and when they turned the corner, he took her into his arms before whispering, 'Great idea of mine, don't you think?'

Jessie whispered back, 'Brilliant idea! Let's head for the cricket pavilion. It's a romantic place.'

'What makes you say that?'

'Oh, just a feeling I have about it.'

It was eleven forty-five when Logan turned the handle on the door of the cricket pavilion. Jessie thought of Maria and her midnight trysts with the gardener. How excited she must have been waiting for her weekly encounters to come around. There was an air of anticipation when walking through the manor grounds so late at night before reaching the haven of the pavilion.

Jessie clung to Logan's arm. 'It's dark in here.'

Logan ran his hand along the wall near the door. 'I'll try to find a light switch.'

Jessie stopped him. 'No. Don't do that; you'll ruin the atmosphere. We can just about see where we're going from the lights outside in the grounds.'

Logan glanced out of a window. 'Don't forget the moonlight. That's helping too. I'm beginning to understand why you feel this place is romantic. Have you been here before?'

Jessie giggled. 'Only on a wet and windy lunchtime, and that time I was on my own.'

Logan bent down to kiss her. 'Well, you're not on your own now.' Jessie closed her eyes as she melted into Logan's embrace. However, she was soon jolted back to reality when Logan pulled away. 'I think we have visitors.'

Jessie's heart pounded at the sight of two torches heading towards the pavilion. 'What are we going to do? How will we explain what we're doing in here?'

Logan took control. 'There must be a fire exit in the kitchen. We can hide until it's safe to make a quick getaway.'

With Jessie and Logan crouching down behind the kitchen units, the main door of the pavilion opened. They heard a man's voice, 'Are you sure all our worries about our jobs can now be put behind us?'

The woman responded, 'Yes. Piers is buying the

place. It's a fresh start for all of us.'

'I doubt he'll need a chauffeur, though. He's already sacked me once.'

'Oh, Charles, you don't need to worry. When I'm his mother-in-law, I'll be able to pull a few strings.'

Charles sighed. 'Are you sure we can't own up to Emilio? It would be such a relief for me if we could.'

'I've told you before; he thinks his father was a pilot. There's no point telling him the truth now. You've always spoiled him in your own way. You made him feel he was destined for better things in life. Just by calling him "Mr Hinchingthorpe", you gave him grand ideas. Thankfully, he didn't turn out too high and mighty. He's kind at heart, it's just a shame he's a bit lost at the moment.'

'Well, I'm worried about him. I'll keep an eye on things, if only from afar.'

'Thank you, Charles.'

Charles held Maria in his arms before kissing the top of her head. 'I must admit, this is taking me back a bit. Remember our Thursday night liaisons?'

Maria rested her head on Charles' shoulder. 'How could I forget?'

Logan could see the whites of Jessie's eyes. He

grabbed her hand and pulled her towards the kitchen door before whispering in her ear, ‘On the count of three, we run!’

Maria was startled by the sound of creaking hinges and a flapping door. ‘Can you look at that door in the morning, Charles? We don’t need unnecessary heart palpitations at our age.’

‘Of course, dear. Whatever you say.’

26

CHRISTMAS EVE IN NEW YORK

Less than a month later, Jessie arrived in New York. Logan had travelled there the week before on business, and she couldn't wait to see him.

Jessie was met with a sea of expectant faces as she wheeled her case through the arrivals area at the airport. It was Christmas Eve, and loved ones were returning home from around the world. Her heart leapt at the sight of Logan waving in the distance. 'Jessie! You made it. You're just ahead of the snow.'

Jessie hugged Logan, who took hold of her case and guided her through the airport. 'We need to get on the road. There's a weather warning for tonight. There's a good chance flights will be cancelled for the next few days.'

Jessie smiled up at him. 'Well, now that I'm here, I'm quite happy to get snowed in for Christmas.'

Logan's eyes twinkled. 'I like the thought of that.'

The journey in a chauffeur-driven limousine through the centre of New York was magical. The couple sipped champagne and admired a city dripping with twinkling lights. The window displays along Fifth Avenue were out of this world, and there was a buzz of excited anticipation amongst children and adults alike.

Jessie turned to Logan. 'Mason and Matty must be excited tonight. I wonder if they'll get to sleep OK.'

Logan checked his watch. 'Well, it's almost five o'clock here, so it'll be nearly ten o'clock in Scotland. I guess their eyelids will be getting heavy by now. They know Santa won't come down the chimney if they're not asleep by midnight.'

Jessie loved the way Logan spoke about his nephews. He knew them so well. Logan pressed a button on a panel in the door to talk to the driver. 'Arnie, can you please drop us off at Tiffany's? I have a present to collect. We'll walk to the hotel from there.'

Arnie responded, 'Certainly, Mr Charteris.' Jessie's heart leapt, and her face became flushed. She'd only bought Logan a bottle of aftershave for Christmas. It was too late now to buy anything else. Arnie parked the car and opened the door for Jessie and Logan to climb out.

Once inside Tiffany's, Jessie was surprised the staff knew Logan by his name. 'Mr Charteris, your bracelet is ready. We've gift-wrapped it as requested.'

Logan took hold of the turquoise package tied with white ribbon and thanked the assistants before guiding Jessie outside and handing her the gift. 'Could you please hold this for a minute? It's a present for Fiona. I'll be in trouble it's late, but I wanted to get it engraved. I'll see her next week, so I shouldn't be in her bad books for too long.' Logan turned around. 'I just need to pop back to the shop; I forgot to wish the staff a Merry Christmas. Wait there; I won't be long.' Jessie felt relieved; her present to Logan of aftershave wouldn't be too bad after all.

When Logan returned, he was rubbing his hands together. 'It's getting colder. I should have brought my gloves.'

A snowflake landed on the shoulder of Logan's black wool overcoat, and Jessie raised her eyes to the sky. 'It's snowing!'

Logan watched as flakes of snow melted on Jessie's upturned face. He bent down to kiss them away. 'I can't remember being as excited as this at Christmas.' Logan swung an arm under Jessie's legs before carrying her down the road and through the foyer of his hotel – much to the amusement of his employees.

Jessie didn't know whether to feel embarrassed or excited. She decided on the latter. Logan was making it clear to everyone in sight that they were together. They'd hidden their relationship back in the UK, but all of a sudden, Logan had gone public that they were an item with one swift move.

A concierge pressed the button for a lift, and when the couple were inside, Logan laughed. 'I've been waiting for weeks to do that.'

Jessie giggled. 'Why were you waiting?'

'Because Mason and Matty wanted Santa to bring you to me. It's Christmas Eve, and they're tucked up in bed. We can tell them they got their wish in the morning. You don't mind about us going public, do you?'

Jessie shook her head. 'Not at all.'

Logan's penthouse apartment in New York was far superior to Emilio's in Paris. Jessie knew she shouldn't compare, but she couldn't help it. Emilio had bought his apartment for secret liaisons with Claudette. He must have wondered why she'd said she still lived with her parents! Jessie then thought about Fanta and Pixie. Logan, on the other hand, had focused on what mattered. He'd concentrated on his career but not at the expense of his family. Just seeing him with his nephews proved that. He was the same age as Emilio but much more mature.

Jessie warmed her hands by the fire in the living area of Logan's apartment, and her heart leapt as the snow through the floor-to-ceiling windows became heavier. Tiny snowflakes had turned to the size of tennis balls, culminating in a thick whiteness on the streets below. A giant Christmas tree twinkled next to a window, filling the room with the aroma of pine. Several wrapped presents were beneath it, and Jessie couldn't help but notice they were all for her. She stood up from scrutinising the labels when she heard Logan approaching. A warm feeling encompassed her. She'd not been so excited on Christmas Eve since she was a child.

Logan smiled at her. 'Have you unpacked? Are you happy with your room?'

Jessie smiled back. 'I'm unpacked, and I couldn't be happier.'

Logan looked out of a window. 'As predicted, we're snowed in. Would you like dinner in the restaurant tonight, or shall we order room service?'

Jessie reached up to brush Logan's fringe away from his smiling eyes. 'Room service would be perfect.'

*

It was one o'clock in the morning when the FaceTime call came from Scotland. Logan woke with a start. He reached for his phone to see a smiling Mason and Matty. 'Santa came! We got everything we asked for!'

Logan made a quick calculation in his head; it was six in the morning in the UK. He tried to sound excited. 'That's great.'

Matty was trying to peer around the corner of Logan's bed. 'She's there! Santa dropped her off!'

Logan turned to see a mop of blonde hair sticking out of the top of his duvet. 'Oh, my goodness!'

Fiona wrapped her dressing gown around herself and tried not to chuckle. 'All I have to say, is that Santa makes everyone's wishes come true.'

Logan coughed. 'Well, almost. He dropped a present for you off at my apartment in New York. I'll have to bring it to you next week.'

Fiona giggled. 'Silly Santa. I'll look forward to that. Now, come along, boys, you've woken Uncle Logan up. He needs to get his beauty sleep.'

27

CHRISTMAS MORNING

Logan had arranged for breakfast in bed. Jessie was horrified. 'I'm so ashamed. What must Matty and Mason think of me? I tried to hide but didn't pull the duvet up enough.'

Logan wasn't concerned at all. 'They're delighted Santa did his job.'

'Well, Fiona won't be fooled. I'm so embarrassed that your sister saw me.'

Logan smiled. 'Why?'

'Because we've only known each other for six weeks.'

'That's long enough.'

'What for?'

'For you to fall asleep in my bed.'

Jessie giggled, and Logan handed her a croissant. 'I know you like these.'

'How?'

'Because the shopkeeper in London said he was surprised you left without buying any that Saturday morning we met in the chilled food aisle.'

Jessie laughed. 'I wanted to make a quick exit. I wasn't wearing any makeup.'

'You're not wearing any makeup now, and you've never looked more beautiful.'

Jessie doubted that, but she was pleased Logan made her feel at ease. She must look a right state, her hair was all over the place, and she was wearing Logan's dressing gown. Jessie remembered the presents under the tree. She needed to go to her room to get Logan's aftershave. 'Well, I'll shower and change straight after breakfast. What's the dress code for today?'

Logan held her gaze. 'Remember when you found Claudette's dress in Emilio's Paris apartment?' Jessie blushed before nodding. She felt bad about telling Logan what happened in Paris but knew she could trust him. Logan continued, 'Well, there's a dress in your room of my New York apartment that was made especially for *you*.'

Jessie frowned. 'I didn't see a dress in there yesterday.'

Logan smiled. 'I sneaked it in there this morning. I've booked a table downstairs in the Larksfield Restaurant for lunch. It's a black tie event, and now that we're in a relationship, I'd like to show you off.'

Jessie had never felt so excited as she reached up to kiss this incredible man. 'Well, in that case, I'll go and get ready!'

Jessie jumped off Logan's bed and ran into her room. The dress on her bed was made from red satin. It was knee-length with long sleeves and a deep v-neckline; it was the perfect Christmas dress. Jessie smiled when she saw the "Antoine Chambray" label sewn into the lining. Logan couldn't have chosen a better present. Jessie would take her time to get ready while relishing a feeling of happiness she'd never known before.

Logan took a step backwards when Jessie walked into the living room. 'Wow! You look amazing in red. I'll be the proudest man alive when we walk into the restaurant together.'

Jessie kissed Logan on his cheek before wiping a red lipstick mark away with her finger. 'Oooops! I can't see this lipstick lasting all day. I'll wipe it off after lunch. Then I can thank you properly for this gorgeous dress.'

Logan's stomach lurched. Jessie was the one – he'd known that from the moment he'd seen her at Antoine Chambray's cocktail party in Paris. His hand touched a small box in his pocket, and he wanted to "seal the deal" there and then. But patience was a virtue, and Logan would know when the time was right to propose to Jessie. It was still early days, and he didn't want to scare her off. Also, Piers had told him to let her fly. An engagement ring may weigh her down. It was a delicate situation, and Logan needed to take his time to get it right.

Jessie handed Logan his present. 'I'm sorry that not much thought has gone into this. I didn't know what to buy a man who has everything.'

Logan unwrapped the aftershave. 'Thank you. It's my favourite, and I don't have everything . . . yet.'

Jessie's stomach somersaulted at that comment, and Logan noticed her flushed cheeks as he bent down to pull a large present from under the tree. 'This is for you.'

Jessie tore at the wrapping paper to reveal a clock with the times of London, Paris, and New York. Logan explained, 'As you know, my hotels are in London, Paris, and New York. When you look at the clock, you will know what time it is wherever I am anywhere in the world. It doesn't matter though if you want to contact me in the middle of the night, my nephews call whenever they want to.'

Logan handed Jessie another present. It contained three paperweights: the Statue of Liberty, the Eiffel Tower, and Big Ben. 'They're for your desk in London.'

Jessie sighed. 'I may not have a desk for much longer. Emilio's forging ahead with selling the business. We're all worried about our jobs. All our agents have meetings scheduled with Samantha Boxtead. Mine's booked in for New Year's Eve. It's rumoured that *The Boxtead Property Group* will take us over in January.'

Logan felt a tremendous sense of guilt. Jessie's job would have been safe if he hadn't put Emilio in touch with Pixie Pettifer. She'd been doing so well at *Rawlinson's Residential* over the last few weeks.

The present opening was interrupted by another FaceTime call. Logan answered it to the sight of Piers and Sophia in the Cotswolds. It was four o'clock in the afternoon in the UK. Sophia waved her hand in the air. 'We're engaged!'

Jessie gasped. 'That's wonderful news!'

Logan's heart sank. Piers had beaten him to it. A proposal to Jessie today was now out of the question. That wasn't a bad thing. Logan would have longer to choose the most appropriate moment. It was, however, comforting to know that Sophia hadn't run a mile when Piers had proposed after a whirlwind romance.

Sophia smiled. 'It *is* wonderful news. Things here couldn't be better. Mamma's happy now she's got her ring back. There's no more mention of ghosts, and Charles has stepped up to the plate. He's let Piers know there are no hard feelings about the "sacking" incident, and he's offered his gardening services as well as chauffeuring. Mamma's talked Piers into keeping him on. Charles has always been part of our family. You should have seen him today with Emilio. Charles bought him a Subbuteo set for Christmas, and they were having a whale of a time before lunch.'

Jessie and Logan smiled at each other before Piers had some news for Jessie, 'Samantha Boxtead called me yesterday, and I praised you highly. Their takeover bid is going through.'

Jessie let out a sigh of relief. 'Thank you, Piers. I've been so worried. I'm meeting Samantha on New Year's Eve. I'll look forward to it now rather than let it spoil Christmas.'

Sophia giggled. 'I'm sure nothing could spoil Christmas in New York with Logan.'

Jessie glanced up at Logan's smiling face. 'You're right. I'm having the best time. It's even snowing! Enjoy the rest of the day, you two. Please give our regards to your family.'

When the call ended, Logan reached under the tree again. 'You have one present left.' He handed it to Jessie, and she unwrapped the photograph of Matty, Mason, Logan, and her with Santa at Hamleys. Logan held Jessie tightly. 'That was the day I knew I was in with a chance.'

Another FaceTime call interrupted the "moment". This time it was Mason. 'Uncle Logan, you'll never guess what's happened.'

Logan widened his eyes. 'What?'

Mason held a keyring aloft. 'I got this in my Christmas cracker. It's got a heart on it. You can give it to Jessie. Mummy says you should put a ring on her finger.'

Logan laughed. 'That ring will be too big.'

Mason frowned. 'But it's the best one I've got.'

Matty squinted, then directed his gaze at Jessie. 'How did Santa get you into Uncle Logan's bed?'

Jessie's mouth fell open, and Logan answered for her, 'Santa brought her on his sleigh.'

Mason had the next question, 'That's so cool. What was it like on Santa's sleigh?'

Jessie gulped. 'Well, it's snowing here in New York, so it was freezing. Luckily I was wearing my hat and gloves.'

Matty smiled. 'I found your glove, *and* I asked Santa to bring you for Uncle Logan.'

Mason wasn't happy with that. 'I asked Santa for a girlfriend for Uncle Logan first.'

Logan stopped the argument in its tracks. 'We have to go now, boys. Enjoy the rest of your day, and don't eat too many chocolates.'

Logan and Jessie waved before Logan turned his phone off. 'We're getting too many interruptions, and I want you to myself.'

Jessie giggled. 'But we're about to go downstairs into a crowded restaurant.'

Logan ran his hand through her hair as his eyes twinkled. 'It may be crowded, but I'll only have eyes for you.' Logan reached for his dinner jacket, and Jessie slid her hand through his arm as they headed for the lift.

28

CHRISTMAS LUNCH

There were smiles from the staff as the boss walked into the Larksfield Restaurant with Jessie on his arm. Logan Charteris was a very private person; this was the first time he'd paraded a partner in public. Well, apart from when he'd entered the hotel yesterday carrying Jessie in his arms – *that* news had ripped through the hotel like wildfire.

The maître d' greeted the couple, 'Merry Christmas, Mr Charteris. Good afternoon, Madam. Your guests arrived early, so we served them canapés and drinks. I've just arranged for a second bottle of Bollinger to be taken to your table.'

Jessie gripped Logan's arm, and he stared down at her in alarm. There must be some mistake. The couple walked behind the maître d' in a daze until they were snapped back to reality at the sight of Guy and Nate, who stood up as Logan and Jessie approached.

Guy spoke first, 'Merry Christmas, you two. I bet you didn't expect to see us.'

Nate looked uncomfortable. 'We hope you don't mind us joining you.'

Logan and Jessie sat down, and Jessie asked the million-dollar question, 'Why are you here?'

Guy rubbed his forehead before knocking back his drink. 'There's no easy way to say this, but Samantha Boxtead has a "last one in, first one out" policy.'

Jessie's mouth fell open, and Logan grabbed her hand. 'What makes you say that?'

Nate took over the conversation, 'Because we've had our meetings with Samantha Boxtead, and they didn't go well. We still have jobs, but we don't want to work for her. She's a force to be reckoned with. She's made it clear that when her company merges with ours, she will need to lose people. Jessie will be the first to go – she'll be made redundant on New Year's Eve. Trust me, the woman's heartless.'

Logan was livid. 'But what about performance? Isn't Samantha Boxtead taking that into account? Shouldn't she be going through a fair and thorough redundancy exercise?'

Guy shook his head. 'We got the clear message it's "her way or the highway". We're gutted. *Rawlinson's Residential* was beginning to soar. Antoine and Giuseppe won't waste their time with the prickly Ms Boxtead – you can bet your bottom dollar they'll take their business elsewhere.'

Jessie reached across the table to hold Guy and Nate's hands with tears in her eyes. 'I can't believe you came all this way to tell me in person. I'll miss you both terribly. When did you get here? Mine was one of the last flights to land before it snowed.'

Nate tapped his nose. 'We did a "Piers". We got ahead of the game. We flew out the day before you to do some sightseeing. It was lucky we did because when we tried to book a table here for lunch, we were told the restaurant was fully booked. We dropped Logan's name into the equation, and the staff were horrified. They thought they'd made a mistake and changed Mr Charteris' booking from two to four. So we got lucky there.'

Guy fiddled with his bow tie. 'We also had just enough time to hire these dinner suits. We didn't plan to dress up as penguins on Christmas Day.'

Nate sighed before turning the conversation back to Jessie, 'That's enough about us; we came here to talk about *you*. We couldn't let you learn about your job on New Year's Eve. Why don't you resign before the wicked witch has the satisfaction of sacking you? You could change your flight and stay in New York with Logan for as long as you want.'

The first course arrived, and the small group ate in silence. Jessie had a lump in her throat that made swallowing difficult, and Logan was deep in thought. Guy and Nate glanced at one another – their "good deed" had turned Christmas into a disaster. Trust them to make a rash decision and follow their hearts rather than their heads. They'd already decided that Jessie wouldn't be the only one looking for a job in the New Year – they'd be joining her. Samantha Boxtead would be losing more staff than she'd bargained for.

By the time the main course was underway, Logan had surfaced from his self-imposed silence. Jessie was pleased that two glasses of champagne appeared to have loosened him up. She tried to keep things in perspective. It wasn't a total disaster; there were jobs out there, and she had much more experience now than when she'd applied for the position at *Rawlinson's Residential*. Jessie was grateful that Guy and Nate had given her the "heads up" about her impending fate – it wouldn't be such a body blow now that she'd had time to prepare for it. The last few weeks had been so exciting and mind-blowing her feet hadn't touched the ground. Jessie had known her luck was bound to change at some point. She just hadn't expected it to happen so soon.

With the main course finished, Logan removed the serviette from his lap and grabbed Jessie's hand. He smiled at Guy and Nate. 'Please excuse us. We won't be long.'

Jessie grabbed her bag from under the table before clinging onto Logan's arm. 'Where are we going?'

'Somewhere special.'

Jessie was surprised when they ended up back in Logan's apartment, and he guided her into his study. 'I love this room. When I sit at my desk, I imagine all sorts of things.' Logan gestured for Jessie to sit in his swivel chair. 'I doodle away and come up with some excellent ideas.'

Jessie glanced at a pad on the desk covered in Logan's doodles. Her eyes caught sight of the words: "*Charteris Luxury Listings*".

Jessie gulped. 'Were you thinking of buying Emilio's business?'

Logan nodded. 'I was, at one stage.'

'Why didn't you?'

'Because I didn't want to scare you off.'

Jessie sighed. 'I can see your point. Our relationship would change if I worked for you.'

Logan smiled. 'Exactly! That's why I've thought of a better solution. It sprang to mind over lunch. When ideas come to me like that, I have to act on them immediately.'

Jessie raised an eyebrow. 'Tell me more.'

'I want to invest in the start-up of *your* business. That way you wouldn't be working for me. You'd be your own boss. However, my idea comes with a catch.'

Jessie's eyes widened. 'What catch?'

'You'll need to change your name.'

Jessie's mouth fell open when Logan opened his desk drawer and took out a turquoise box tied with white ribbon. He handed the box to her. 'I didn't go back into Tiffany's to wish the staff "Merry Christmas" I needed to collect your ring. I had it sized the same as Maria's. That one fitted your wedding finger. Giuseppe knew what size it was from when it was valued. Why don't you open the box to see if Giuseppe gave me the correct information.'

Jessie's heart pounded as she untied the white ribbon and opened the box. Another turquoise box was inside, and she handed that to Logan. 'You open it.'

Logan sprang the lid open and took out a large solitaire diamond ring. He knelt down on one knee before smiling up at Jessie with sparkling eyes. 'Will you marry me, Jessie? If you do, I'll be the happiest man alive.'

Jessie was shaken to the core. Could this really be happening? She opened her mouth, but no words came out. She could see Logan's concern at her hesitation. His handsome face was crumpled with frown lines. Why hadn't Jessie been prepared for the happiest moment of her life? She knew why – she'd never believed in fairy tales – until now. What could she say, or do, to alleviate the awkwardness?

Jessie took a tissue out of her bag to wipe her red lipstick off before holding out her hand. 'Of course, I'll marry you. What took you so long to ask?'

Logan let out a sigh of relief, before sliding the ring onto Jessie's finger and lifting her out of his chair to kiss her. After placing his fiancée's feet on the ground, he had another question, 'Does this mean you'll take on the role of Head of *Charteris Luxury Listings*?'

Jessie smiled. 'On one condition.'

'What's that?'

'I want Guy and Nate to come and work with me.'

Logan shrugged. 'You can do what you like with *your* business. I can see why you'd want to employ Guy and Nate, though. They're good guys who must think the world of you to fly to New York to give you bad news.'

Jessie reached inside her bag and pulled out her lipstick. She applied it as she spoke, 'Well, let's get back to the restaurant and turn bad news into an amazing new venture.'

Logan reached for his phone. It was still turned off. He'd resist breaking the news to Fiona and the boys until he arrived in Scotland with Jessie. There was no need for her to return to London for a while. Until the new business was up and running, they could spend time together planning their future.

Jessie caught sight of her reflection in a window as they headed for the lift. She couldn't believe this was all happening. She was on Cloud Nine and never wanted to get off. Jessie glanced up at Logan, smiling down at her. She brushed his wayward fringe away from his twinkling green eyes, the sparkles from her diamond ring darting around the room. At that moment, Jessie realised she was the luckiest girl in the world.

29

A NEW VENTURE

Six months later, *Charteris Luxury Listings* was open for business with its office on the ground floor of Logan's London hotel. Jessie had invited old clients, and potential new ones, to an event to mark the occasion. It was the end of June and perfect weather for an afternoon tea party on the hotel's roof terrace. Jessie couldn't have managed without Logan's investment and the free use of office space until the agency was established. Then there was Piers – he was invaluable as a mentor. Even though Sophia was three months pregnant, Piers was always available to offer Jessie advice and guidance.

Guy and Nate couldn't be happier. They'd suffered working for *The Boxtead Property Group* until Jessie's business was up and running. Now they were all back together, there would be no stopping them. Antoine and Giuseppe were the first clients on the books of *Charteris Luxury Listings*, and Giuseppe had changed his website to recommend the new agency's services.

With the party in full swing on the roof terrace, Jessie took time to count her blessings. She went down in the lift to the ground floor and unlocked the door to her office. Looking around, she could see the photograph of her and Giuseppe in Rome on the wall – Guy and Nate had removed that from *Rawlinson's Residential* before Samantha Boxtead took over. Next to the photograph was the clock Logan had given her on Christmas Day. It was now three o'clock in the afternoon in London, four in Paris, and ten in the morning in New York.

Jessie sat in her swivel chair, and her heart lifted at the sight of the Statue of Liberty, Eiffel Tower, and Big Ben paperweights. Souvenirs of the three cities that had "sealed the deal" for her relationship with Logan.

The phone on Jessie's desk rang. She picked it up. 'Good afternoon, Jessie Charteris speaking. How may I help you?'

The voice down the phone sounded like velvet. 'My name's Gregor. I'm calling from Caracas.'

Jessie sat forward in her chair, her heart thumping. 'What can I do for you, Gregor?'

'I have properties to sell.'

Jessie hated to admit it, but there was no way her new business could take on work in Venezuela. She took a deep breath before responding, 'I'm very sorry, but we're focusing on properties in the UK at the moment, with a view to expanding into Europe.'

Gregor articulated his requirement. 'I have three houses in London's West End. I want to sell them and buy something larger – nearer to Buckingham Palace so I can see the Changing of the Guard. Antoine said you would sort me out.'

Jessie's heart leapt before responding, 'Well, in that case, we can help you. Let me take your details.'

One hour later, Jessie had a new client. She felt guilty she'd left Guy and Nate alone on the roof terrace entertaining the guests. But Jessie guessed that was the way things would go in future. She needed to delegate, and who better to delegate to than people she could trust?

Jessie re-arranged the paperweights on her desk and then studied the two photographs in pride of place. One was of the day Logan "knew he was in with a chance". Jessie smiled at Matty and Mason standing rigidly in front of Santa and her and Logan looking awkward from behind.

The other photograph was of her wedding day to Logan. They were married last month with a large family gathering at a castle in Scotland. They hadn't run through any heather, and Logan hadn't worn a kilt. But that didn't matter. It had been a beautiful spring day, and the castle grounds were carpeted with bluebells. Mason and Matty were page boys and well-behaved during the ceremony and wedding breakfast. They were back to normal in the evening and running around the castle playing hide and seek. With Logan relieved of childminding for the day, Fiona was run ragged. Jessie smiled at the memory – it had been a wonderful day.

The door to Jessie's office opened, and Logan strolled in. 'It's going well on the roof terrace. Guy and Nate are doing you proud.'

Jessie stood up before sliding her arms around her husband's waist. 'I only popped down here for a quiet moment to take in the enormity of what we're doing. I won't get many quiet moments in future.'

Logan ran his fingers through his wife's hair. 'I'll make sure you get quiet moments; don't you worry about that.'

Jessie rested her head on Logan's chest. 'I've just taken a call from Caracas. Antoine put a new client in touch with me.'

Logan smiled. 'The world's your oyster, Jessie. I'm very proud of you. If you want to go global with your office base, my Paris and New York hotels are at your disposal.'

Jessie pushed her husband away before laughing. 'Go steady! London is enough for me at the moment.'

Logan pulled her back into his arms. 'London will always be our base and the townhouse our retreat. It's good to take time out from work. I've been guilty of not doing that enough in the past, but I didn't have someone to share the quiet times with until now.'

There was a knock on the office door before it opened. 'May we come in?'

Guy and Nate entered with a bottle of champagne and four glasses. Guy popped the cork, and Nate explained their interruption, 'We needed a quiet moment. Piers and Emilio are entertaining everyone on the roof.'

Jessie raised her eyebrows. 'Emilio's here?'

Guy nodded. 'He certainly is. He said he wouldn't miss it for the world. Emilio's not a fan of Samantha Boxtead. He's said he'll do anything he can to help us get *Charteris Luxury Listings* off the ground.'

Jessie smiled before frowning. 'That's so kind of Emilio, but I'd question why he'd sell his business to her if that's the case?'

Guy raised his eyes to the ceiling. 'They were

having a fling in December.'

Jessie choked on her champagne. Over a short period of time, Emilio had gone from Fanta to Claudette, to potentially Jessie, back to Fanta, and then on to Pixie Pettifer. Then he'd fallen into the arms of Samantha Boxtead! Jessie had been lucky in more ways than one. She'd had a lucky escape from an immature man who couldn't make up his mind.

Jessie frowned. 'Dare I ask who Emilio's brought with him today?'

Nate sipped his champagne before responding, 'He's with the chauffeur from Hinchingthorpe Manor. We were surprised to see them walk in together. Piers and Sophia travelled here on their own.'

Jessie glanced at Logan. 'Well, that's very kind of Piers to lend his chauffeur to Emilio. Charles has known the Rawlinson family for years.'

Guy topped his glass up. 'Well, they certainly seem very familiar. I could have sworn Emilio called the chauffeur "Papa".'

Nate frowned. 'I think that's what Emilio's been missing. He's lost his way for a thirty-two-year-old. If the chauffeur can offer him fatherly advice, that's a good thing.'

Logan winked at Jessie before changing the

subject. 'I'd like to propose a toast to your new business.'

Guy put his glass down on Jessie's desk. 'Wait a minute! I meant to do this earlier.'

Nate grabbed Guy's glass. 'I'll help. Come outside into the corridor, everyone, and bring your drinks.'

Guy pulled out a reel of gold ribbon and fixed it across the doorway of their new office before handing Jessie a pair of scissors. 'Ready. You can do the toast now, Logan.'

Logan's eyes twinkled. 'All great things have small beginnings. I wish you every success with your new venture. Here's to *Charteris Luxury Listings*!'

Jessie walked up to the gold ribbon before cutting through it to cheers from the small group. She turned to smile at Guy and Nate. 'And may we have fun along the way!'

Guy high-fived Jessie, then Nate. 'That's a given! It's only a matter of time before we get a new client. Someone in the world must be keen to work with us.'

Jessie chuckled before responding, 'There is. He's in Venezuela.'

Guy gulped. 'My bag's packed. Tell me more.'

'Gregor is coming here next week, so there's no

need to pack a bag. Come along, you guys. We should go and help Piers and Emilio out. I'll lock the office and meet you on the roof.'

Guy and Nate finished their drinks and then headed for the lift. Jessie turned to Logan. 'I have a good feeling about this.'

Logan smiled down at his wife; she'd never looked more beautiful. Her pale blue eyes were bright and sparkling with excitement. He bent down to kiss her before responding, 'Me too.'

****

Printed in Great Britain
by Amazon